the

implacable

order

of

things

JOSÉ LUÍS PEIXOTO

TRANSLATED FROM THE
PORTUGUESE BY RICHARD ZENITH

the
implacable
order
of
things

NAN A. TALESE | DOUBLEDAY
NEW YORK LONDON TORONTO
SYDNEY AUCKLAND

PUBLISHED BY NAN A. TALESE

AN IMPRINT OF DOUBLEDAY

Translation copyright © 2007 by Richard Zenith

Published in the United States by Nan A. Talese, an imprint of The Doubleday Publishing Group, a division of Random House, Inc., New York

www.nanatalese.com

Originally published in Portugal as *Nenhum Olhar* by Temas e Debates, Lisbon, in 2000. Copyright © 2000 by José Luís Peixoto. This translation was first published as *Blank Gaze* by Bloomsbury Publishing, London, in 2007.

DOUBLEDAY is a registered trademark of Random House, Inc.

LIBRARY OF CONGRESS CATALOGING-IN-PUBLICATION DATA
Peixoto, José Luís, 1974–
[Nenhum Olhar. English]
The implacable order of things : a novel / José Luís Peixoto ; translated from the Portuguese by Richard Zenith.
     p.   cm.
I. Zenith, Richard. II. Title.

PQ9316.E59N4613 2007
869.3'5—DC22

2007037272

ISBN: 978-0-385-52446-9

PRINTED IN THE UNITED STATES OF AMERICA

1 2 3 4 5 6 7 8 9 10

FIRST EDITION IN THE UNITED STATES OF AMERICA

the

implacable

order

of

things

book one

TODAY THE WEATHER DIDN'T
fool me. The afternoon is perfectly still. The air scorches, as if it
were a waft of fire and not just the air we breathe, as if the afternoon refused to die and the hottest hour had begun. There are
no clouds, just wispy white streaks unraveled from clouds. And
the sky, from down here, looks cool, like the clear water of a
dammed stream. I think: perhaps the sky is a huge sea of fresh
water and we, instead of walking under it, walk on top of it; perhaps we see everything upside down and the earth is a kind of
sky, so that when we die, when we die, we fall and sink into the
sky. This sky that's a bottomless stream without fish. The clouds
just hazy threads. And the air an inwardly burning fire. Hot,

invisible flames that make our skin swelter. Air that, like a tired man, doesn't even stir.

A time will come when not a sparrow can be seen, when nothing can be heard but the silence of everything watching us. The time will come. I'll see it on the horizon. As surely as I realize this now, I realized it yesterday when I entered Judas's general store and ordered my first and my second and my third glass. I realized that all across the plain the cicadas and crickets will fall silent. The slenderest twigs of the olive and cork trees will stop climbing into the sky; from one moment to the next they'll turn to stone.

IT WAS NIGHT WHEN JOSÉ ENTERED Judas's general store. He still wore sun-bleached clothes on his body, the earth's ochre light on his skin, and a reverent smile on his face. He was preceded by the blunt, dirty tip of his shepherd's staff. His tired sheepdog, a new mother whose swollen teats and bloated belly almost touched the ground, followed him. He set down the sack that was slung over his shoulder by a rope and leaned against the counter. A glass of red wine. The few men who greeted him muttered languishing, indecipherable syllables. The others, without interrupting their talking and drinking and card playing, merely turned their heads to look at him. The dog rested her ribs on the ground, curved her spine in an arch of vertebrae showing through her fur, and lowered her eyelids over her passive brown eyes.

In the moment that José raised his glass and downed the wine in one fell swoop, the men in Judas's general store as seen from the other side of the square, as seen from the night and from silence, were the open space of a doorway; they were a tenuous path of light trying to advance across the vacant square and the black, black night; they were a place of indistinct words trying to enter the vacant square and the black, black silence. José set his empty glass on the counter, and next to him, under the dim light and the racket of words, the devil's idle smile instantly took shape. The devil smiling. He was the only one who didn't have sun-darkened skin, whose shirt was ironed, trousers creased, hair combed between his cap and his slightly protruding horns. He was the only one who smiled. Two glasses of red wine, he ordered with a smile. José didn't need to look at him. In silence he waited for the two glasses that were filled to the absolute brim. While they drank, the devil didn't take his eyes off José, and he seemed, even while drinking, to smile a faint smile that divided and multiplied into a thousand smiles, a thousand faint smiles. The men continued, or seemed to continue, their unending conversations and unending card games, stopping only to glance at the changes in José's face and at the tempter's taunting grin, or to spit out the damp remains of their hand-rolled cigarettes. And José's face changed. Successive glasses gradually filled him with an irrational happiness, the happiness of carnival and masqueraders. The devil smiling. With a smile he asked how are you, I haven't seen your wife around, where is she? José's eyes flared, and he stopped tittering to answer she's where she should be, where she always is. The men's crisscrossing voices were now an ocean of words rolling in waves over their heads, waves that began with a drone and swelled in a far-reaching din before retreating, leaving behind vestiges of words in the air, worthless and jumbled-up syllables like old things in a compost pile. Always? asked the devil, smiling and laughing. José fell silent, and the men fell silent to hear the answer he didn't utter. Two more glasses of red wine, the devil insisted. You know, he went on, still smiling, the giant told me that he knows her better than you do, that he knows better than you where she is, where she spends her time. From the white distance of his alcoholic aura José stopped to grasp the words. Under the hovering dust the men opened their tiny eyes like moles and tried to laugh but didn't know how, they just grunted. I'm sick of that giant's lies, José answered; my wife is where I know she is, where she always is; the next time you see him, tell the giant to show his face, tell him to show me his face. And he raised his fist high, striking it long and loudly on the counter. The dog got up and slowly walked out. Tell him to show me his face, José repeated, and I'll smash it in. The men's expressions froze for a moment, and then, as if on cue, they all started to dance in unison, whirling in a circle around José. And José, who could barely make out their blurred outlines and colors, once more radiated happiness in his face, and he whirled and danced, fell and fell, and stood up to dance again. In a corner the devil smiled, finally satisfied in his smiling.

THIS SILENT WAITING UNNERVES ME. The last sheep has lain down next to the curled-up bodies of other sheep, beneath the big old cork tree. I think: men are sheep that don't sleep, sheep that on the inside are wolves. The sun is still sun, its fire persists, in the air's and the earth's slow combustion. In the same shade as me, leaning against the same trunk, my staff resembles a person eyeing me with pity. My dog, in front of me, occasionally lifts her heavy gaze, likewise aware of what's going to happen.

THE DOG SOLEMNLY WALKED AHEAD of José's uncertain steps, stopping now and then to wait for him. The sky overhead became darker, blacker, once they were outside the town and on the sand-covered road leading to the farmstead, the Mount of Olives. The din of the men's shouting in Judas's general store continued to sound in José's dazed head. In the night's scant clarity his silhouette was that of a strange animal with three or four legs, depending on whether he was propped up by his staff or crawling on all fours. Plodding forward in this way, he began to be suspicious of the scrub and underbrush in the ditches. One moment he would attack the brush and its invisible phantoms with his staff, slugging away at himself on the ground; the next moment he would start running and feel his suddenly enormous feet trip over each other.

From the fence that bounded the farmstead he saw the sun rising over the roof of the rich people's house. Like the darkness, the alcohol in José had slowly dissipated and given way to light. He regained his clarity of mind and once more felt the weight of sobriety. Looking into the sun, José paused to collect his certainties of what lay ahead. He stood there awhile. Then climbed the slope. Once they'd passed through the gate, the dog relaxed, making her way to the washtub and plopping down underneath it. José's house, whitewashed and with yellow trim, lay a few yards beyond the rich people's house, at the back of the courtyard, behind the waterwheel and a small garden that the rich woman liked to see kept up. With his eyes fixed on the front door of his house, José walked through the yellowed garden, pushed aside the beads, and crossed over the threshold. In the night that still lingered in the bedroom, without breaking the silence generated by the presence of things, José made out his wife on the bed and remembered the devil's smile and the devil's words. His wife's head against the pillow, her hair against the pillow, were what he had conquered and were also what eluded him. He turned to the crib, and his gentle movements became even gentler. His son's innocent face glowed in José's breast and in his tender gaze. Looking at his own hands, he suddenly felt that they were too rough to touch the baby's soft, smooth skin. Obsessed by the certainty that gnawed at him and gnawed at him, he went back outside.

He whistled and his dog stood up, rejuvenated. He untied the knot of wires that secured the gate and felt the dog pass between his legs. As the sun at the foot of the sky became stronger, the dog made the sheep leave the pen in a steady stream, and the ones in front, who knew the way, dragged an ever-larger cape of slender bodies behind them, an ocean tide of shorn sheep flouncing in the new morning.

THE WORLD HAS COME TO A STANDSTILL, in a picture where I can only keep going, where my staff can only continue, where I can only keep whittling this broken branch with my jackknife, where my staff can only continue to stand watch over the plain like a venerable old man.

The birds have all flown away. The animals of the ground make no sound. The clouds have all halted. The moment is near at hand. I look into the sun and think: if the punishment that's my lot can be contained in me, if I can accept it and somehow hold it inside me, perhaps I'll be spared further judgments, perhaps I can rest. The loud roar of silence surges behind the earth. The fire of the horizon is approaching. And I see him. He walks straight toward me with mechanical steps. His body, larger than a man's, is like that of a walking tree, like that of a man the size of three men. And each of his steps is equal to three human steps. Beneath the cork trees, the sheep have become lifeless, curled-up balls of wool. Closer now, he looks at me without veering his gaze. Still closer, the rage in his eyes grabs me and slowly pulls me toward him. Right in front of me, he stands perfectly still. We look at each other.

THEY LOOKED AT EACH OTHER. Sitting beneath a tall cork tree, José held his open knife and a whittled piece of branch. Leaning against the same tree, to his right, was the staff. The giant's unwavering frame blocked the sun and cast a shadow that ended in the round shadow of the tree. Within the silence, as within a dream, the giant began to walk. José looked at him as if waiting, as if a great amount of time had passed during those two long strides, and he felt three successive kicks in the gut, and he didn't defend himself. He didn't reach for his staff, he didn't tighten his grip on the jackknife. The giant opened wide his huge hands and flung him to the ground. José looked at him and didn't shrink when the giant's toe-plated boots began to maul his flesh and crack against his bones, kicking him in the back, in the hips, in the shins. The moments that passed in silence and that seemed like an entire night to José were not a night, they were just a few moments within the silence. The sweating giant turned over José's inert body, and despite the blood and dirt that smeared his skin, José's gaze was the same. The giant felt like thrashing him some more, thrashing him until that gaze disappeared, but instead he turned around and walked away, without once looking back. José's abandoned body was like a bush or stone or some other object that the wind slowly sweeps from the landscape. The singing of the sparrows and crickets and cicadas increased. José looked straight at the sun. His hand still held the open jackknife.

· · ·

9

PERHAPS A SLIGHT BREEZE has kicked up and the leaves of the cork trees are trembling, like the hands of old people. My body feels crumpled, indented by the bumps in the ground where it lies, submerged in the earth's frozen waves. Perhaps the birds and animals have come back, to look at me. I see the sun before me, high above me, like a god embracing me with rays of light or of death. I think.

T HE THREE MEN WERE LEAN-
ing against one of the large tanks of olive oil. There were four
such tanks, square and very tall, with spigots at the bottom. Under the four spigots were four pails that received, at precise inter-
vals, the tiny shout of dripping oil pierced by a clean, clear light.
It was summer in the hot hour of that summer's day, but there,
in that dusky room of the oil press, the summer was hot only in
the placid imagination of the three old men; beneath the roof
tiles and within the cold walls of old bricks thickly coated with
lime, their forgetful bodies remembered cool weather. It was
summer and little oil remained in the iron tanks, but the smell
that had accumulated over the years wafted in the air, wrapping

and penetrating and blending with the old men's heavy words. Old Gabriel, seated to the far left, looked down as he spoke, lifting his eyes only during the brief silences. Under the black shirt of a very black mourning, his tanned skin was covered by the thick white of an undershirt. Above the cobwebs of his thick beard's whiskers, his face was marked by a prophetic profusion of wrinkles and by a gaze as large as a pond. He rolled his cap over in his hands.

HE LOOKED DEAD WHEN I FOUND HIM. Day was breaking in the window when I heard his wife knock on the door. I had a clay mug of milk on the fire and didn't drink it. She said he took the sheep out yesterday and didn't come back, I spent all night worrying, unable to sleep. She doesn't talk much. She chooses her words as if choosing oranges from the lower branches, or the healthiest pups from a litter. She said where could he be? Help me. That morning she talked more than usual. Which is perhaps what made me think she was right to be worried. If José hadn't taken out the sheep, I'd suspect that he'd drunk too much and lost his way returning from Judas's general store to the Mount of Olives, but he did take them out, and knowing José as I do, from the time he was a boy trailing behind his father, catching crickets and setting traps for the sparrows, I can say, I can guarantee, that only a serious problem would keep him from meeting his obligations. My boots made a dragging sound in the sand. As I walked, I listened and knew that something had happened. He looked dead when I found him. His neck was twisted into a sullen grimace, and his body, stretched out on the ground, was like an inert stone, born there and molded by a strange fortuity into the exact shape of a man. His dog, relieved of the work of keeping all the sheep together throughout the night, ran to me like a child telling me everything. She licked my hands while I petted her on the head. José, like a dead man, kept staring at the sun with his glassy, wide-open eyes. I leaned him against the tree with the help of the dog. Unable to carry him, I went to the farmstead to fetch a wheelbarrow. As I walked up the slope, I couldn't avoid his wife, who looked at me hard and read my face. She was no longer interested in him but asked how he was, waited for my answer, and returned to her silence, alone. With his legs and arms hanging out of the wheelbarrow and almost touching the ground, José kept his eyes open the whole way. Ahead of us the dog drove the flock. José stared at the sun like a dead man, each beat of his heart raising just slightly his shirt.

TO THE RIGHT OF OLD GABRIEL sat the two brothers with their parallel gazes, fixed on abstract, unfocused points. Their gazes were equal but didn't see the same thing. They were the same gaze, seeing two different things. During the months when the oil press was idle, it was the brothers who looked after it. Always together, always at each other's side, they had aged simultaneously: they had the same curve in the back, the same halting gait, and, although they didn't know it, the very same number of white hairs on their heads. Many more than seventy years had passed since the clear August morning when together they emerged from their mother's womb, ripping her up inside. Old people told the story, which they'd heard from their parents, of how the mother, as soon as the umbilical cords were cut, looked and saw that they were Siamese twins. She died, without a word, a few minutes later. It was considered to be a terrible tragedy, and the whole town attended her funeral. Everyone expressed to the father their condolences, both for his wife and for his twin sons, for no one imagined that children like that could thrive. But as their mother was being buried, the babies slept under three folded blankets in their father's bedroom, next to the bed where their mother had bled and perished. The babies slept, their skin all wrinkled, with their joined hands lying on top of the sheet that covered them, as if innocently proud of being brothers. And under the watchful eye of the people around them, they grew up as children do. As they got older, many people looked closely at their hands and were astonished by what they saw: the right hand of one and the left hand of the other were joined by a common little finger. They had very elegant hands, with long and slender fingers, but from the last knuckle of their pinkies, the two fingers were fused and ended in a single fingernail. Everyone who saw this thought of ways to separate them, but the most adamant of all was the man who pulled teeth with pliers. Waxing enthusiastic, he claimed to know men who had amputated many legs and arms in the war, and he said that he'd read a lot of books, complete with diagrams, and that cutting a child's finger was easier than pruning a grapevine. The father of the brothers asked him but how am I to decide who to leave without a finger? And the man who pulled teeth with pliers promptly answered that he'd already thought of that problem: the fairest thing would be to cut the finger off both of them. The father of the brothers glared at him for a moment and never spoke to him again.

The brothers were called Moisés and Elias. If you looked straight at them, Moisés was the one on the left, Elias on the right. For obvious reasons, Moisés was right-handed and Elias left-handed. Except for that detail, they were absolutely identical. But although they were absolutely identical, moved together in perfect harmony, and were indistinguishable to the naked eye, there was a difference that divided them or, perhaps, united them all the more: Elias didn't talk. Or rather, he talked only into the ear of Moisés, who would, when necessary, immediately give voice to his brother's whispered words. That's how it had been since they were children. Some people swore that they'd caught them talking by surprise, exchanging words in a primitive, perhaps foreign tongue, a quasi-animal language. This had never really been proven, but in the hazy penumbra, in the cool, cool shadow cast by the tanks in the scant light, that's what happened. Elias whispered some incoherent sounds into his brother's ear, and Moisés listened and repeated out loud what his brother had said.

I NEVER SAW ANYONE more eager to get married than José. The night before the wedding, we were in Judas's general store, and his wide-open eyes laughed the whole time. Everyone there knew it was a laugh that wished to hide many things, that wished to hide the giant and all the rest. He wanted to marry and he got married, but he was never able to forget what had happened to his wife, because no one else ever forgot, because his wife never forgot, because people when they talk to him are careful not to mention his wife, careful not to mention the giant.

I remember his wife when she was still a little girl, when her father was still alive and worked at the brick kiln. At that time, in midsummer, we would pass by in our wagon at the crack of dawn, on the way to the tract of Senhor Tomé, and her father would already be drawing buckets of water from the well and working the clay with his hoe or kneading it with his feet. At that early hour there were already molds filled with clay and a stack of bricks drying in the still-cool sun. And since she had no mother, she was there too, in her filthy dress, a friendly little girl, and she'd run up to the road, wish us a good day, and hitch a ride for a few yards on the back of the wagon. At day's end, on our way back to town, we'd see her father in front of the kiln, sweating as if his skin were water, as if his skin were the skin of a river, he'd be in front of the kiln, placing bricks in rows amid the flames and embers. She, with her dress now even filthier, would again come up to us, wish us a good day, and hang on to the end of the wagon. At the top of the road, when we reached the turning, I'd look back and see that lone man, working amid the flames, and that little girl, gleefully running around the brickyard.

ELIAS STOPPED TALKING INTO MOISÉS'S EAR, and the silence, which was there even while he spoke, was now all that the three old men's faces expressed. For a moment, the oil that dripped into the pails reechoed with importance. For a moment, the shadows. And it was the voice of Moisés, now speaking for himself, that softly sounded, as if his lips weren't even moving, so soft and tenuous and fragile was his voice.

BEFORE HER FATHER WENT TO THE GRAVE, we went to see him at home, coughing coal and ashes onto the bed, onto the sheets. I remember that it was on a Sunday and in September. He was in an iron bed that screeched with a jolt every time he coughed. José's future wife was a skinny girl, of some sixteen years marked by hunger and want. She ran this way and that, slithering between us, as if something she did could save her father from dying, as if her bringing a clean towel: a towel she'd scrubbed and scrubbed against some stones and dried in the sun: as if her bringing a towel could save her father, who coughed clouds of smoke and spurts of blood as if coughing his lungs out; as if her bringing a glass of milk: milk that she begged for and someone said no, that she begged for and someone else said no, that she begged for and someone gave it to her saying don't ever come back here: as if a glass of milk could stop him from burning up inside and throwing everything up including the glass of milk.

She ran this way and that because her father was all she had. It was in September, in the afternoon. Her father still wasn't in the grave, and already I noticed how from time to time the giant would pass by on the street and crouch down to peek through the window.

B EFORE MY FATHER WENT TO
the grave, the brothers came to see him. What I most remember
is how those brothers, hooked together by a finger, were always
in the way. I'd turn to the left and find one of them, I'd turn to
the right and find the other one, or the same one. I'd return to
the bedroom with some warm milk and run up against the back
of one or the other, I'd step to one side and be up against an
identical back, I'd step to the other side and still the same back,
until I'd eventually manage to slip past. Those brothers were like
paper dolls joined at the hands, like inseparable dolls condemned
to a perpetual line dance. And my father, slowly dying, and I
knowing that he was slowly dying but not wanting to believe it.

My father, who was all I had, wasting what energy he had left to say tell me how the brickyard's doing. Slowly dying and asking about the kilns and the well. The brickyard that wasn't his but that belonged to him more than to Doctor Mateus, who never hauled a bucket of clay, who never touched clay with his hands or feet, who never saw clay. Go and take the rent to Doctor Mateus, sweetie. And I, under the blazing sun, would walk to the Mount of Olives clenching a sweaty banknote in my fist. Finding José there, I'd say here's the rent money for Doctor Mateus, and José, without even looking at me, would put the banknote in his pocket. On my way back, now more relaxed, I'd stop under the cork trees to cool off, and I'd think about the pretty sadness of José's eyes. Reaching the brickyard, I'd find my father looking at me in the same way he looked at me before dying, enclosed in a silence of not being able to say what he felt and saying it in a speechless stare. I remember the brothers just sitting there, like vultures on death's branches, and the massive waist of the giant passing back and forth outside, visible through our flimsy tulle curtains. And my father, silent for prolonged moments, as if meditating on something that only he knew and only he could know, with the same gaze I now see in José, looking straight ahead at nothing. José who, unlike my father, isn't going to die but who seems to know secrets reserved for the dying. José, lying between the sheets I washed yesterday, all beaten up, his chest wrapped up in a bandage, gazing the way angels on church altars gaze, with wide-open eyes. Wrapped up in a bandage, because yesterday I called for the bonesetter, who, after cracking his knuckles in a symphonic scale, poked his fingertips into José's flesh. He ran his hands over his back and neck, probing to see if anything was missing, and when he reached his ribs he said whoa, I looked at him and he repeated whoa. Then he silently dug his fingers deep into José's chest and, after a crack that echoed, said if I hadn't pulled out that rib, it could have punctured his lungs. I paid him, and he left José wrapped up in a bandage. But his gaze hasn't changed. Does he think I'm a gaze-setter? The baby fell asleep a while ago, so now I could rest up a little, but I've been feeling anxious. This bedroom reminds me of my father's bedroom when he was dying, and I even have the impression, perhaps by way of suggestion, that the giant's hulking figure has passed by the window. Back and forth. Like on the day after my father died, his body still fresh and intact under the ground, the worms still not having discovered it but already gnawing at my heart and filling it with grief, the terrible grief of having a dead father, just that one father, just that one person suffering for me and hurting for me and caring about me, and that person no longer existing. On the day after the end of my childhood, the giant knocked on the door and didn't repeat in a weary voice the usual words of sympathy, chanted like a litany or a curse; he looked at my skinny body and hugged me. Just like that. He hugged me and lifted me in the air and squeezed me hard. Again I was a little girl in her father's arms, spinning around in her father's strong arms and smiling in a world made only of mornings and springtimes, a tiny girl who could smile. And on top of the sheets my body ripped and torn as if by the fangs of wolves, my torn body opening up in a gush of blood that didn't gush. On top of the cold sheets of my father's bed, sheets like marble, on top of that coldness, the absence of my blood. And the giant, on top of me, saying you whore. Into my ear: you whore. And the bedroom ceiling melting into tears, becoming a night sky in the night. I who had never been with a man or experienced anything like that having to hear, each time the giant's volcanic respiration warmed my ears, you whore, in

20

gusty breaths: you whore. At the foot of the bed, he buttoned himself up and stared at me, smiling. And I, on top of the sheets, like a broken doll with its hair sticking out, its arms separated from the trunk, its legs yanked loose, its head twisted. The next night the giant returned, and the next night, and the next night, and the next night. I would open the door without looking at him, I'd lower my head, and in my father's bedroom I'd feel him going through me with a knife. Every night the ceiling would open to show me the stars that didn't exist in the nocturnal sea of those nights. When my period didn't come and I fell out of sync with the moon, I said nothing to the giant, since he never heard my voice, since I've never to this day spoken to him. My belly grew quickly. After fifteen days, it looked like I'd been carrying for two months; after a month, like four months. When the ice-cold forceps dug inside me, I stopped feeling. I stopped hearing. I stopped seeing. I know that the old woman with rough hands and false teeth was wearing a plastic apron. I know they stretched me out on a hard bed, as on a slaughtering table. I know they stuck a clay bowl beneath me to catch the blood, like the fresh blood of pigs, stirred with a wooden spoon to keep it from coagulating. But I saw nothing, heard nothing, felt nothing. Deaf and blind, I didn't even imagine the child that was yanked out of me like a tumor or a hex. It was as if a fog had entered my life, penetrating to my bones and blinding me to what doesn't exist: mornings, clear skies, spring, and your embraces, Papai. And I was no longer a child. At home, at night, the giant didn't return. In the street, wrapped in my black mourning shawl, I walked very close to the buildings. Conversations stopped when I came near, and the women or the men stared at me, as if their eyes were probing me, as if they wished to humiliate me with their eyes, as if their eyes were saying you whore, as if their eyes were my conscience that never stopped following me and repeating you whore. By the time of the olive harvest I still hadn't found work and was living off what my father, in between the solid flakes of smoke he coughed over his asthmatic words, passed on to me: precious little. By the time of the olive harvest, Doctor Mateus's oldest housekeeper died of old age, worrying as she died about Master Mateus's breakfast, because for her Doctor Mateus, married and with many sons, was still the little boy whom she'd lovingly helped deliver on linen sheets. I trudged over the paths leading to the Mount of Olives, asked to fill the vacancy, and was hired on the spot, even before Doctor Mateus had eaten his breakfast. And José, who now looks dead but isn't, for I know the smell of death and it's very different from glassy eyes meditating on a personal condemnation, José sometimes came by when herding the sheep or when carrying armfuls of firewood, he and his father, to the rich people's house. At the time old Gabriel was around a hundred years old and tended the vegetables in the garden. I spent the days shut up inside. At night I slept with the other housekeepers on iron beds in the attic. None of them would talk to me. I never again saw Doctor Mateus, who stopped coming to the farmstead. Sometimes postcards for the doctor's wife would arrive from foreign cities, cities that I invented from the strange photographs of a huge building ending in a point or of a building that was leaning and about to fall, cities that I invented until the cook shouted shut up. Postcards arrived for the doctor's wife, but she had likewise packed all her bags and left. We were alone, but we did everything as if the rich people were still there. And it was then that, while dusting, I began to hear a voice shut up inside a trunk. A trunk that was old and polished, like all the other trunks, like everything else in the rich people's house, old and polished, a trunk in the main hallway, beneath a portrait with a handlebar mustache, and inside the trunk a voice. At first I thought it was a person shut up inside, but the cook, one afternoon when the muffled voice talked to me, said pay no attention, it's just a voice. It talked in a solemn tone, as if it were reading an epic poem from a book, saying: perhaps people are, perhaps they exist, with no explanation for it; perhaps people are pieces of chaos on top of the disorder they enclose, and perhaps this explains them. I couldn't ignore the voice shut up inside a chest. It was a man's voice. On the week following this discovery, I pretended to have work to do in the main hallway so as to listen to the voice. It said phrases that seemed very true to me, but I never answered, and the voice shut up inside a chest perhaps wasn't even aware of my presence, though I began to consider it a friend. I would stand there listening and nod my head yes or fix my gaze on the ideas it raised as if it were raising horizons. When the other housekeepers saw me doing nothing, they'd push me out of the main hallway toward the kitchen. The cook would put the wicker baskets in my hands and send me to town on an errand. And through the wheat fields, under the cork trees, I'd follow the sandy, sunlit road to town, and when I arrived I'd walk very close to the buildings, and the groups of women and of men would scrutinize, with their gaze, my shrinking figure, and as I passed by I'd hear she had an abortion, I'd hear abortion and feel even more ashamed, hugging the building wall even more, as if I were a sheet of paper stuck to it. At the grocer's I didn't say what I wanted, I handed over the piece of paper with the cook's illiterate handwriting, and everything was loaded into the baskets. I went a roundabout way to avoid the square, but I never escaped the devil, who was waiting for me on a corner, in the shade, smiling. And beneath that smile my legs got tangled, like basting, my legs turned into plasticine, and with baskets under my arms, on my head, and in my hands, I was like a drunk circus performer sliding along a high wire. It was as if the devil's gaze had stripped me of everything, of all the building walls behind which I hide from others and hide even from myself. When I reached the beginning of the road, I was already tired. Loaded down like a mule of the Gypsies under the midday sun, I sweated and silently cursed the cook. In the coolness of the kitchen, I felt as if I'd crossed many deserts, and I was given five minutes to refresh. With a piece of cardboard I fanned my face and the neckline of my dress. On the crooked chair, I opened my legs and felt the relief of a breeze against my raw, burning thighs. In those days the voice shut up inside a chest, always changing, said: perhaps suffering is tossed by handfuls over the multitudes, with most of it falling on some people and little or none of it on others.

I THINK: PERHAPS SUFFERING
is tossed by handfuls over the multitudes, with most of it falling
on some people and little or none of it on others. Not pain, not
my legs made stiff from black bruises, not my smashed ribs sticking together amid squished blood, not my head splitting like
lightning into tentacles, not the skin of my thwarted passions
opening up gashes as if from the blows of an absolute impotence,
but suffering without respite, as if all my bones were exposed
and piercing through my muscles and skin. My body hurts, and
I suffer without feeling it. I know that my wife is pacing around
the house. Our little boy has fallen asleep, she could rest if she
wanted, but she's anxious. She paces around the house, and I

don't know what she's thinking. I don't know her. I see her always as if for the very first time. Without hearing her, without feeling her, watching her movements that belong to no story I can grasp. I've often contemplated her small, girlish forehead and her deep gaze, but I've never been able to pass through her walls, which have no doors or windows into her essence, I could never walk through her rooms and light them up with a lamp, however dimly, however faintly. I'm as ignorant about her as I was on the day I decided that I wanted to know her.

AT THE TIME OF THE OLIVE HARVEST, when José's wife began working at the rich people's house, she had the body of a skinny and tired child. She walked from one corner of the house to another. With drooping shoulders that prolonged her neck, she was a thin blob to whom orders were given. Neither José, nor the other housekeepers, nor the cook, nor old Gabriel, nor anyone said anything to her or heard her utter a word, an exclamation, a sigh, a whisper, a breath. But whenever any of them got into one of the wagons that take field workers to and from the town, whenever they went to the square and into Judas's general store, people asked them about her and said abortion, they all said: she had an abortion. And neither José, nor the other housekeepers, nor the cook, nor old Gabriel, nor anyone else replied.

Two summers later the cook, sick of preparing steaks and stewed lamb and steaks and stewed lamb, sick of seeing the steaks and stewed lamb get cold on the table without Doctor Mateus to pull back his heavy chair made of dark wood and leather and without Doctor Mateus to sit down and fill his glass of wine and sniff it and hold it up against the light and only then perhaps drink it, sick of seeing steaks and stewed lamb get cold on the table without the doctor's wife to place a napkin on her lap with the embroidered coat of arms facing upward and without the doctor's wife to sit down or even to arrive from the empty bedroom where she no longer slept, sick of seeing the platters of steaks and stewed lamb get tossed into the food for the dogs, decided to quit the farmstead and go live in a whitewashed house in town. And in the moment the cook took her leave, waving a farewell handkerchief to the farmstead and dragging picnic baskets tied with string and stuffed with flannel underpants to the wagon, in the moment the mules got tired of waiting for the cook as she wept over fifty years of service in that house, in that moment the housekeepers suddenly realized that they too were sick of making and unmaking and making and unmaking the beds already made up with the clean and ironed sheets of their employers, sick of dusting the furniture in the living room without the doctor's wife reclining in the chaise longue and scolding them for not doing anything the way she, sitting in the chaise longue, ordered, sick of dusting the furniture in the hallway without Doctor Mateus sneaking up from behind and grabbing their breasts and breathing down their necks as their hearts jumped in fright. Suddenly sick of it all, the housekeepers rolled up in a handkerchief what they had in the drawer of their nightstand, because everything they owned fit into the drawer of their nightstand and into a handkerchief, and seized the opportunity to leave with the cook, who was grateful for their company. And neither the cook nor the housekeepers noticed José's wife, camouflaged by a clump of mallows. The girl from the brickyard, who from that morning on took charge of the rich people's house.

She cleaned the rugs when they were dirty, she dusted when there was dust, she didn't make the beds since they were always made, she waxed the stairs if they needed waxing, she didn't prepare steaks and stewed lamb, since housekeepers were only allowed to eat bread soup with an occasional egg added. She kept the house without expecting the owners to arrive at any moment, for there was no reason to think they would arrive at any moment. She spent her afternoons sitting next to the voice shut up inside a trunk, listening. Now and then she'd go into town on foot with the shopping baskets and she'd hear abortion, she'd hear: she had an abortion. And on her way home, before leaving the town, she'd cross paths with the devil, who looked at her and smiled, and smiled.

José would accompany his father, or perhaps by this time it was his father who accompanied him. José was twenty-six or twenty-seven years old, and his father even older than his seventy years. José's mother, bedridden, had died of a disease that made her wilt like a flower that gets yellower and yellower until she was just yellow and dead, a disease that had begun in her breasts and took over her whole body. The whole body of José's mother was that disease. José's mother died of a disease that was her whole body and she died on a Saturday afternoon, in the middle of a sweltering summer. José's father became even older, as if with the passing of that afternoon and that moment in which his wife died, that precise moment when her heart stopped on a beat and left her chest waiting in an unremitting silence for the next, unarriving beat, that exact moment when she failed to breathe in again and her head fell in obedience to her muscles' last will, as if with the passing of that afternoon his age had doubled, making him almost as old as Gabriel, and even deader. José couldn't suddenly age like that. On that same afternoon he had to take care of the sheep and take care of the funeral. The next day, after the funeral, he again had to take care of the sheep. And again the next day. And the next day, the next day, the next day. José's father didn't return to the farmstead. He stopped talking and only ate spoon-fed soup. José's sister, married to the blacksmith, lived in town, and she was the one who took their father in. Just look how pathetic, she said to the neighbor women. Their father would sit all day long on a stool in the backyard, in front of the chicken coop, looking at nothing, like a blind man. One day a week the barber would come by full of chitchat, good morning, wrap a towel around his neck and shave his beard, talking all the while, because of this and because of that, blah-blah-blah, believe it or not; every three weeks or so he would take a pair of scissors from his smock and cut José's father's remaining hair almost down to his scalp, talking all the while, because of this and because of that, blah-blah-blah, believe it or not, although José's father was completely indifferent. His other most frequent visitor was José, who would sit next to his father, the two of them in silence. And José realized that, although they had spent day after day together driving the herd and seemed, at night, to have spoken a great deal, they'd never really said much to each other. And they sat there side by side, facing the chicken coop, as if the afternoon were what they wanted to say.

Without his father to help and with Doctor Mateus abroad, José found himself in charge of the properties and business concerns that the doctor maintained there; he was like a steward, though no one called him that. But these new responsibilities didn't change his routine. He continued, as always, to tend the sheep, which was his main task. Sometimes he went into town to visit his father. Or to visit the cook. Or to stop briefly at Judas's general store for a glass of red wine. It was during one of those brief visits that the devil appeared, smiling and greeting everyone there. José drank the rest of the wine in his glass and turned to leave, when the tempter smiled at him and asked about the girl who was to become his wife, saying so how is the girl from the brickyard doing? José said just fine, but he didn't really know how she was doing, he just wanted to answer without answering and to go away. But all the men in the store were looking at them and listening. The devil, with a seemingly nervous smile still stuck on his face, said I hear that she hasn't forgotten what she did and that she'd like to do it again as soon as the right man comes along. José walked past the men and their gazes and said, at the door to the general store, that's her business, not mine, and left.

Early next morning, José knocked on the door of the rich people's house and paid more attention to the sad and inexpressive face that opened it. And while he walked through the kitchen, carrying armfuls of oak wood and rockrose branches, he looked at her as if for the first time, at her arms, her fragility, her white skin. And when the morning had become fully morning and one could feel the sun's warmth, José hid behind the waterwheel to spy on her hanging laundry from the clotheslines. Slender and delicate, she set down the basket, and José was enchanted by that slender, delicate figure who, imagining herself alone, passed amid the bright whiteness of the hanging sheets and blended in with it, since her skin was also white and reflected the sun. Later, when he let out the sheep and drove them to pasture, he dreamed the whole time of that skin and its white brightness. From that day on he wanted to know her.

I THINK: PERHAPS SUFFERING is tossed by handfuls over the multitudes, with most of it falling on some people and little or none of it on others. I suffer. I know my wife is pacing around the house. I don't look at her. I look at the sun in the sky over the house. I see through the ceiling and the roof tiles. I look directly at the sun. And at its light. Like a river current, it rushes in, fills and purifies me. And beyond this current that washes me as if it were water, not light, I know that my wife is pacing around the house. Even though my eyes don't see her, I see her. She's thinking. What are you thinking about, wife? Who is that face of yours? And no silence answers me. There's only the silence which I don't understand, in which I don't hear her. Only a silence of forgetting and of indifference and of silence. Far from this shaft of sunlight and close to my skin she's pacing around the house, perhaps lost, perhaps sure of what she knows. I need her. I don't know her.

JOSÉ'S WIFE MUST HAVE BEEN about twenty and would spend long hours sitting in a chair in the main hallway, listening to the voice shut up inside a trunk. José, who must have been about thirty, had the blindness of looking out for her and noting down what he saw in a notebook: the day, hour, place, and description of each sighting. Wednesday, nine thirty a.m., garden, asked old Gabriel for some collard greens, slender wrists. Thursday, eight fifteen a.m., courtyard, went into town. Saturday, quarter to noon, fed the chickens, I heard her voice. José tried to discover her routine so that he could wait for her or follow her more easily, but she was as apt to wash the laundry in the morning as in the evening, she didn't have a set day for going into town, and she fed the chickens whenever it occurred to her. José suffered on her account. When he woke up, at the crack of dawn, she was the first thing he thought of. As he tended the sheep he thought of her. Sometimes he couldn't see her face, worn down from him having imagined it so much. Then he would tightly shut his eyes and construct her piece by piece, remembering her lips, nose, hair, and eyes, and then he'd combine all the parts in his mind.

He'd think of her as he went to sleep. When he spotted her he
felt his heart beating faster in his temples.

He kept this up for enough months to fill a dozen notebooks.
But she knew he was watching her, she was perfectly aware of
the feeling that was consuming him, not because she'd ever
caught him and not because she had some supernatural power
but because she was a woman and all women know more than
they see, when feelings are involved. And one day, late in the afternoon, the light was dwindling in a luminosity that hung over
the fields, spreading across the plains and across the world, since
the world ended on the horizon of the plains; one day, late in the
afternoon, she crossed the courtyard, walked by the waterwheel
and the small garden that the rich woman liked to see kept up,
and knocked on the door of José's house. When he opened it,
she looked into his eyes, and his face, in an instant, became profound. And she was the one who broke that instant, silently
passing through the beads that hung across the threshold. José
followed her. And they went into the bedroom and made love.
And not feeling the weariness of her frazzled body after its last
exertion of the day, she quietly left.

The next day, after quickly grazing and penning up the
sheep, José went into town. In his sister's backyard he found his
father in the same chair as always, like a marble statue getting
old. José sat down and, after an hour, said I'm going to get married. No change occurred in the faces of the two men. After another hour had gone by, he was already making the necessary
arrangements for the wedding. He got married three weeks later.

It was on a Saturday in July. José wore his only suit, a black
suit that had belonged to Doctor Mateus and that was baggy in
the sleeves and big in the waist, a black suit that he'd used for his
mother's funeral and his sister's wedding. The bride wore a white

dress that had belonged to the doctor's wife and that she recovered from its use as a floor rag. They were married by the devil, he being the one who performed the town's weddings. The two male witnesses were Moisés and Elias, and the two female ones the cook and the madwoman from the Rua da Palha, since she happened to be passing by the church door and was pulled inside. The guests were old Gabriel, José's father, José's sister, his brother-in-law the blacksmith, and his seven-month-old nephew. Dressed in lay clothes, the devil entered behind the altar and, smiling, began to read from a black book. José's forlorn father sat in a corner, stiffer than the agonizing wax figures. His sister, with a bunch of plastic tulips on her head, rocked her baby back and forth like a broken clock, and the child's cries echoed in the church like an air-raid siren. The cook, out of sorts, muttered through her teeth. The madwoman from the Rua da Palha drooled and jerked this way and that, like a bullock besieged by blowflies. The devil, saying nothing, smiled wide. José said yes. His bride nodded her head. The witnesses signed with an X, except for the madwoman from the Rua da Palha, who signed with a scribble. No one was waiting outside the church. No one threw flowers. There was no lunch or reception. Everyone went home. That night José's wife slept with him, but they didn't make love.

On Sunday José had to tend the sheep. The young bride, with the indifference of a wife married for twenty or thirty years, made coffee and went to wash the laundry in the washtub of the rich people's house. José didn't go spy on her.

I THINK: PERHAPS SUFFERING is tossed by handfuls over the multitudes, with most of it falling on some people and little or none of it on others. Even if I feel a great weight on my chest, doesn't an abyss weigh more? Even if I feel like a blind man advancing without eyes toward a precipice, I have to get up from this bed. I have to raise these arms that aren't mine, I have to raise these legs that aren't mine but those of a huge rock, and go tend the sheep. My sheepdog. The fields. The big old cork tree. What shade is cast by the big old cork tree? Even if in midafternoon I'm walking in the night, even if the sun at its height is the blackest night, and inside night there's just more night, since everything is night to my eyes, I have to get up from this bed. Even if it's just to suffer and suffer, I have to go face what I'll be next, since that's what I'll be and I can't escape it, I can't escape becoming something.

WRAPPED UP IN A BANDAGE, José got up and began to get dressed. His wife looked at him and said nothing. The baby woke up.

T HEY REMAINED QUIET, THE
three old men, for a long time. The walls of the oil press were
covered by a layer of lees, like a protection against the cement's
roughness. The color of the men's faces absorbed the darkness
of the oil press. Quiet, all three. Moisés, Elias, and old Gabriel all
thinking of one thing and thinking that the others were thinking of another thing, but they were all thinking the same thing.
Moisés was thinking of José's wedding and of the cook whom he
met that day; he thought that Elias was thinking of José's wife
when she was still a girl at the brickyard and that old Gabriel was
thinking of José's wife hidden away at the Mount of Olives, already worn and used. Elias was thinking of José's wedding and

of how that was the day his brother fell for the cook; he thought that Moisés was thinking of José's wife when she was still a girl at the brickyard and that old Gabriel was thinking of José's wife hidden away at the Mount of Olives, already worn and used. Old Gabriel was thinking of José's wedding and of how Moisés had pulled his brother by the little finger, almost pulling it off, so that he could get closer to the cook at the altar; he thought that Moisés was thinking of José's wife when she was a girl at the brickyard and that Elias was thinking the same thing as his brother.

Moisés was thinking of José's wedding and of the cook, whom he met that day.

IT WAS ON A SATURDAY IN JULY. My brother and I wore our newest suits and our jackets with navy buttons that were the last thing the tailor made before he died, for he didn't want to die without leaving us each a suit for special occasions, and he was the only one capable of inventing and executing an intricate system of buttons and fasteners and straps that would allow us to wear shirts, sweaters, and jackets. Since it was Saturday, we woke up a little late, at eight thirty. We drank our coffee and put two clay pots of water on the fire. When they came to a boil, we grabbed them with a rag, since clay also burns, and poured them into two enamel tubs in the middle of the kitchen. We added a tad of cold water and took a bath. We shared the blue soap and dried off with the same towel. We sat on two stools by the fire and clipped our fingernails and toenails. Our suits, ironed the night before, hung on the chairs in the bedroom, next to our shined shoes and brand-new socks. It was Elias who ironed them, for he has always been more delicate with his hands, and the suits, albeit the newest ones we owned, were made when we

36

were young, and any carelessness with the weight of the hot iron could scorch them permanently. I remember Elias asking me to move the iron around and to stir up the embers, and this I know how to do. Since we don't have much beard, we merely sprinkled some scented water on our cheeks and let our two or three fine whiskers, white or blond, have a chance.

Outside, the day was the bright sun flooding the building walls and the ground and sky, turning everything, walls and ground and sky, into a sun as well. We walked without a care and, as I remember, smiling. It seemed, like all Saturdays, to have good things in store. The frightened chickens scurried out of our path. The dogs looked at us in a friendly way. People said good morning to us. We reached the church and the door was closed. On the three front steps José's sister was holding on to her baby, who whined as if he wished to fill the morning air with the deafening bugle sound of his screaming, while José's sister talked nonstop in a torrent of scarcely intelligible words: look what I have to put up with the sun beating down on us and no one showing up to open the door and no bride or groom look what I have to put up with this kid who won't shut his trap I only just fed him I just changed his diaper he just woke up and already he's whining to go to sleep: rapid words without letup, like a wailing or a lament; the blacksmith was leaning against the façade, hunched over and downcast, smoking a cigarette and staring at the ground; José's father, looking hypnotized, was squatting like a child on one of the church steps, with a strip of cloth tied around his neck. We said good morning. No one answered us. There was nothing to do but wait, and it was truly uncomfortable. The sun hotter and hotter. The baby screaming at the top of his lungs.

When the devil arrived, we wiped the sweat off our foreheads

with our jacket sleeves. And while he fiddled with the key, we
lined up behind him. The dejected blacksmith went over to José's
father, gently lifted him up, and led him by the strip of cloth that
he wore against his will around his neck, like a leash. Which in
effect is what it was. The blacksmith sat him down and untied
the cloth from his neck. We sat down. The baby kept screaming,
and it seemed impossible that such a tiny body could have a
throat strong enough to scream like that. The devil, forever smiling, walked around the altar getting things ready, and we saw
everything, since the church has no sacristy. He struck an entire
box of matches that went out as he tried to light a candle, he
tasted a moldy host, he donned a chasuble that came unstitched
at the back, and as he continued in these preparations, she arrived. She appeared in the doorway to the church, lit from behind, and that silhouette dazzled me immediately. I knew that
she had moved into town, but I still hadn't seen her. During the
fifty years she'd worked at the Mount of Olives, I'd never once
seen her, since whenever I went to the farmstead, she was busy,
and whenever she came into town, we never chanced to meet.
But I knew that she'd moved. I even knew that she'd moved next
door to the house of the man who writes in a room without
windows, and during the months since then I'd often invented
excuses for us to pass that way when coming home from the oil
press. Even so, I never saw her until that moment when she entered the church. Although it was very hot, she wore a maroon
velvet dress and some lace-trimmed stockings that covered her
shins. She walked in front of the altar and didn't make the sign
of the cross before the tabernacle. In fact no one made the sign
of the cross before the tabernacle, not only because no one
knew how to make the sign of the cross but also because the
church had no tabernacle. She stole along the aisle by the wall

and sat down right next to me. She grumbled about the heat and the discomfort of her clothes, and she didn't say good morning. Hot and sweaty, she waved a fan which, I found out later, the rich woman had brought her from the fair in Seville.

The groom entered hand in hand with the bride. The cook pulled the madwoman from the Rua da Palha into the church, saying help us out here. The baby boy of José's sister howled. Given the position of the bride and groom at the altar, it fell to me to be a witness for José. The cook refused to be a witness for the bride, muttering abortion, muttering she had an abortion, so she ended up next to me, as a witness for the groom. Muttering, she passed on to me the scent of her perfume. She was a woman. As was plain to see from the way she took a hanky from her purse and blew her nose, from the way she moved her lips while chewing on tiny words, from the way she impatiently shifted from one foot to the other. She was a woman. And it didn't fluster her to see me and my brother attached. And she almost smiled at me once. And she almost looked into my eyes. She was a woman.

ELIAS WAS THINKING OF JOSÉ'S WEDDING and of how that was the day his brother fell for the cook.

THE CHURCH WALLS WERE MADE OF ROUGH STONE, though successive layers of whitewash had smoothed them down somewhat. On each side there was a saint, regarded as such just because they were there and not because they were really saints, for no one knew who they were. And the ceremony proceeded. Smiling, the devil read phrases, intoning them like a chant, while my brother was falling in love with the cook. There were also two small stained-glass windows. The floor was made of wood and riddled with worms. José's sister's baby wouldn't quit bawling, he didn't even stop to breathe, he bawled incessantly, and although we heard the devil chanting a lament, we couldn't make out the random words. The madwoman from the Rua da Palha, who was a witness with me for José's wife, had a large stain of drool on the front of her sweater and a huge bloodstain on her skirt. She didn't wear stockings and her legs were filthy black. Her hair was all disheveled and fleas crawled on her neck. She moved her body in almost controlled jerks, and her head twisted to see something in the air, something I tried to see but couldn't, something that flew and made her head move every which way on her neck. The screams of José's sister's baby ricocheted against the church walls until it became impossible to distinguish between the shouts coming from the child's open mouth and red face and the identical shouts repeated by the walls. They shouted at the same time, walls and child, shouts coming at us from all sides. The cook blew her nose continuously. Before her hand could get from nose to handbag with her colorful, flower-stamped hankie, she would be sniffling again, and we could hear the full depth of her sniffling in spite of the baby's shrill cries. And my brother looked at her with rapture. The cook muttered, as if praying. With her small mouth she muttered softly, quickly. As if she were eating grains of rice, one by one, or slurping soup from a spoon, with an annoyed, irate look, almost a look of hatred. And my brother looked at her with rapture. The cook restlessly shifted her weight from one foot to the other, perhaps because her shoes pinched or perhaps because she was irritated by the screaming child or by the madwoman from the Rua da Palha who smelled like manure. And my brother looked at her with rapture. The moment arrived for exchanging rings, and the bride and groom had no rings. Unconcerned about this detail, they placed imaginary rings on each other's finger. My brother didn't see this, for by then his eyes were glued on the cook. As if he were stuck to her and not to me. As if she were a woman.

OLD GABRIEL WAS THINKING OF JOSÉ'S WEDDING and of how Moisés had pulled his brother by the little finger, almost pulling it off, so that he could get closer to the cook at the altar.

MOISÉS GOT CLOSER AND CLOSER TO THE COOK, defying the laws of observation, for it seemed that the closer he got, the better he could look at her and size her up. As if, leaning his shoulder into her and twisting his neck in a bundle of tendons and thick veins to look at her from within one inch of her ear, almost burying his nose in her hair, he could better appreciate her; as if his shoulders were eyes that saw; as if two eyes focused on a fuzzy, badly defined ear were the same thing as seeing a woman at a distance, seeing her walk and seeing her pass by us and draw away while we think about her, which is also a way of seeing her. And he solemnly continued, with twisted neck, to focus on that ear that wasn't even very pretty, or very feminine, or well shaped. And the farther he pulled away from his brother, the more one could see how complicated were the jackets they wore. On the inside of the sleeve common to both and in the waist area beneath that sleeve there was a row of laces with wide bows and concealed buttons. Except for that, they looked like elegant jackets. Stately blue in color, they were furnished, in front and on the cuffs, with thick, anchor-embossed buttons of imitation gold. They were made of good cloth, and whitish stains marked the place of the shoulder blades. Moisés got closer to the cook and pulled his brother with him. Pulled him like a dead weight by jerks that he pretended not to notice, Elias seeming concentrated

41

on the wedding and on the devil's smile and on the madwoman
from the Rua da Palha and on the saints with faded written notes
from remote civilizations stuck with safety pins to their moth-
eaten gowns. The bride and groom, cut by the horizontal line
of the two brothers' outstretched arms, stood with their backs to
the nave, while the broadly smiling devil faced it. He read from a
book and smiled. He wore an old chasuble and smiled. At a certain point he held the book in front of them and said they should
kiss it. They didn't kiss it. José's sister's kid was screaming and,
by this time, was screaming inside our heads. An echo inside an
echo of a voice inside a voice inside our heads. And we hardly
heard, or we didn't hear at all, the long question asked by the
quietly smiling devil, but the silent question hovered, suspended,
in the devil's inquisitive and suspended gaze. José said yes. His
wife nodded her head. When the witnesses were asked for their
signatures, Moisés was surprised to see the cook pull away and
walk off; perhaps he thought she was a statue that sniffled and
blew its nose. The kid kept screaming. Outside José's sister, with
a bunch of plastic flowers on her head, talked with the profusion
of a cartload of oats being dumped into an empty storehouse:
grains on top of grains in the air, without letup, words on top of
words, like an open faucet of oats or of words, one grain after
another and before it, one word beginning in the middle of the
previous word and that one finishing and the next one only half
said when another one begins, and so on. The devil smiled all
alone. The madwoman from the Rua da Palha stood in a corner
of the churchyard, amid the dust and stones. The churchyard was
all dust and stones, as every street in town was dust and stones,
and amid the dust and stones she stood and, separating her legs,
began to urinate, the faint whistle of her bladder and the foamy
puddle of urine. José's father was like an ancient tree, withered

or almost dead, whose sap ran deep and slow. The newlyweds took their leave, and no one congratulated them or had anything to say to them. They took their leave and disappeared with little more than a few murmurs. Without the bride and groom, we suddenly realized there was no reason for us to be gathered there. The blacksmith took the strip of cloth from his pocket, tied it around José's father's neck, and left with his wife and baby. Through the streets of the town they carried the kid's screams, which diminished, though on certain curves they could still be heard loudly, and sometimes a stray wind or a memory would bring them back from afar. And the cook left. And Moisés tried to talk his brother into following behind her. They followed. It was midday. The madwoman from the Rua da Palha, left all by herself, wandered about the churchyard.

THE EVENING FELL LIKE A SCREEN IN THE SKY over the oil press. The three old men maintained their silence.

HROUGHOUT THE REST OF
the summer, the brothers often passed by the cook's house.
When it was already late, after nightfall in August, they would sit
on the stone bench outside the house of the man who writes in a
room without windows and remain there all evening. At the beginning of the street, there was a nook with a fountain, and from
there to the end of the street all the doors were open, and the
people who lived there sat in the doorways. The man who writes
in a room without windows was the only exception, he never
came out, and so Moisés took advantage. Night after night, for a
whole week, he had to convince his brother to go there, but then
it became a habit and there was no more need to convince him.

Moisés talked loudly with the migrant who lived opposite the cook and sometimes talked with her, softly. It so happened that Elias sat on the side of the cook, which meant that Moisés and the cook had to talk either in front of him or behind him. No one said anything to Elias. Elias said nothing to anyone. And the warm night, the cook's dull chatter about pennyroyal and purslane, the stars, the cool trickle of water falling into the shallow pool of the fountain, all made Elias fall asleep. And he only woke up when someone passed by on the street. He woke up with a zigzag of good evenings: good evening here, good evening there, good evening here, good evening there. Moisés didn't fall asleep, and even in bed the thought of the cook kept him from sleeping. In September the days began to get shorter and a bit cool, and the brothers were the last to quit the ever-cooler evening coolness and the stone bench of the house of the man who writes in a room without windows.

The sun of late September was almost as hot as the sun of August, but the season for sitting in the doorway at night had passed, and Moisés and the cook stopped seeing each other. But Moisés was the kind of man who won't give up, and one day he thought: it has to be. The next day he again thought: it has to be. The day after that he again thought: it has to be. And two weeks later he contrived to meet the cook at the door to the grocer's. They got married on a Saturday, the date of which they forgot. Since the cook's house was larger, it was the two brothers who moved. They loaded three wagons with chests and junk. They rented out their place for not very much money, but it helped pay expenses.

The brothers weren't big spenders. They had the clothes they needed, and what they earned from the oil press was enough for them to eat platefuls of boiled potatoes with collard greens and lots of olive oil for lunch and dinner. The cook, who for all her adult life was used to tasting the rich people's food at the Mount of Olives, wouldn't settle for collard greens. If at first she made collard greens and potatoes in all the ways collard greens and potatoes can be made, soon she used her expertise to obtain new ingredients. In the first weeks she made boiled potatoes with collard greens; the brothers sat at the table and ate up. Then she started making pies and empanadas out of potatoes and collard greens; the brothers sat at the table and ate up. After a month had gone by she made sculptures out of potatoes and collard greens that sighed like women in love and seemed to blow thick-lipped kisses from the collard leaves, green lips dripping olive oil from the corner of the mouth; Elias, somewhat warily, and Moisés, eagerly, sat at the table and ate up. One night for dinner the cook placed, in the middle of the table, a platter with shapely, wide-open potato legs and an open, steaming vagina made of collard greens which, by a trick of her culinary art, slowly contracted before the brothers' eyes, contracting until it became a collard-green vagina that was irrevocably closed and dried up, with just a trickle of olive oil; Elias, feeling perplexed, and Moisés, perturbed, sat down and ate. Moisés and the cook looked at each other in a silent understanding, and the next morning he ordered turnip greens and onions from old Gabriel. On Sunday morning the brothers set traps for the sparrows on Gallows Tree Hill. Some days later Moisés bought two packages of noodles; then he picked out some good mushrooms; then he bought half a pound of shark's meat; then he went acorn picking; then he planted garlic and cabbages in the backyard; then he grew parsley and coriander in a tub; then he raised rabbits and hens in a chicken coop he built out of crates; then he bought three sardines; and then he bought some fruit. The rent money from the brothers' old house began to go entirely toward food.

I THINK: PERHAPS THERE'S A LIGHT INSIDE PEOPLE, perhaps a clarity; perhaps people aren't made of darkness, perhaps certainties are a breeze inside people, and perhaps people are the certainties they possess.

JOSÉ, AFTER HE GOT MARRIED, didn't talk to his wife straightaway. They walked to the farmstead without holding hands, in silence. Across the expanse of the sunlit plains José and his wife trod, and beads of sweat trod over them, on their skin. Across the expanse of the sunlit plains went José and his wife, dressed as bride and groom, illuminated. When they reached the farmstead and the house, José didn't remove his suit and his wife didn't remove her dress. He put the black sheepskin on his back, grabbed his staff, and went to tend the sheep. She donned a rag that served as an apron and went to wash two already washed plates. At night they slept in the same bed but didn't touch each other.

They continued to sleep in the same bed, because they were married and married couples always sleep in the same bed, because they had only one bed, because only one bed fit in their bedroom, but they didn't touch each other again. And summer came. The passing days were long, as days full of sun and still with hope naturally are, with a vast and ordered sky whose blue has the depth and simplicity of being the blue of sky and sun and continued hope. The passing days were long, and José, in those days, was a new man with a serene face, hoping and yearning for a future, yearning each day for the next day. José's wife continued to harbor a silent sadness, the sadness of a deep well containing all sadness; she continued to care for their house and for the rich people's house. And with the door locked from inside and the keys in her pocket, she would sit for entire afternoons listening to the voice shut up inside a chest. And in these moments she almost let herself smile. She looked sad to José, but he didn't know what to think. She looked sad, but he couldn't tell if she was tired or sick or nervous or angry or indifferent or sad. She looked sad, but he got used to the mystery of her sadness and didn't wish to change her. He was very fond of her. Sometimes, among the sheep, he would single one out, or he would single out a tree when among trees, and he'd call it by his wife's name. Out loud. And he'd see that name scatter into the air and vanish in the clarity. Alone in the fields, he'd repeat that name and see it hover for a few moments. He'd repeat it and stand still, smiling. He'd sit down in some shade, smiling.

On the last night of summer, as he'd always done on the last night of each season since turning eighteen, José went to the house of the blind prostitute. Prostitute was a word left behind by a traveler and used by the townspeople to baptize the blind prostitute. It was a strange and difficult word that twisted around the tongue and that the townspeople only used when referring to the blind prostitute, but it was an apt word, because it wasn't the word whore. The blind prostitute wasn't a whore, she was a woman, sad because blind, who did favors since there was nothing else she could do. Her mother had been just like her and her grandmother had been just like her, but it was said that her great-grandmother had been a fickle baroness who abandoned her daughter among some brambles. Abandoned her for being a girl. Upon seeing her for the first time, still smeared with her blood; upon seeing her and regretting she wasn't the boy whom she had imagined and for whom she'd bought a complete set of baby clothes in Lisbon; upon seeing her for the first time, she'd said she looks like a whore. People say that the scars from her grandmother still mark the womb and back of the blind prostitute. They say that the thorns blinded her grandmother and remained inside her to blind whatever daughters she might have. The blind prostitute's mother had been blind. And the blind prostitute had a blind daughter. A one-year-old girl who rarely went outside. Pretty because tiny, and blind. The blind prostitute wasn't a whore, and José went to visit her on the last night of summer. She lived on the Rua da Palha, and when she heard three knocks on the door, she was already expecting him. For his sake she had lit a very faint kerosene lamp, and through the darkness tainted by a dim clarity she led José to her bedroom. Through the open door of the bedroom the weak lamplight entered even more timidly, and by that light José could make out the body of the baby lying under the sheets. It was the tiny body of a girl with long black hair and, beneath her missing eyelids, the cavities of her eyes. Perhaps she was sleeping. Without talking or making noise, they got undressed and lay next to the little girl. They made love, each one probing the other's body, becoming the other's body. José washed himself in the basin that was in the kitchen and left money on the rustic wooden table. On the road to the farmstead, under the night sky, José thought of the blind prostitute's eyes. They were two deep cavities of smooth flesh the color of bright blood. Two blood-colored cavities in the face of that woman.

The next day, the first day of autumn, José, when he woke up, wanted to see his wife's eyes and to see her get dressed. Lying down, he noticed her belly. He got close and ran his hand over her belly. It was a hard mound, rising above her navel and making his hand rise as it passed over it. They looked at each other, and the sun that was in the morning entered the bedroom. José tended the sheep and went into town. In his sister's backyard he sat down next to his father. They sat there all afternoon, and in a moment no different from the others, he announced I'm going to be a father. José kept looking at where he was looking. José's father kept looking at where he was looking. The afternoon slowly hung there, indifferent to all this.

I THINK: PERHAPS THERE'S A LIGHT INSIDE PEOPLE, perhaps a clarity; perhaps people aren't made of darkness, perhaps certainties are a breeze inside people, and perhaps people are the certainties they possess.

THAT SAME WEEK MOISÉS MARRIED THE COOK. Both were more than seventy years old, but both conserved a pungency salted by many summers, by seventy summers. Elias was his brother's male witness. The other witnesses were paid. No one was invited to the wedding. Moisés and the cook slept in the same bed and touched each other. Winter was already bringing a breeze that, in the early morning, could be called chilly, when Moisés brought home a basket full of oranges. With remarkable dexterity Elias peeled oranges with just one hand, using one finger to secure the rinds, another to remove the seeds, and a third finger to hold on to the seeds, and he separated the segments one by one, eating them with evident relish. The cook looked at them more intently than usual, but they suspected nothing. On the dining table flowers cut out of carrots and tomatoes blossomed from inside a lettuce salad, flowers that sprouted among the lettuce leaves and formed a bud that opened up in a magnificent flower. On the platter a little woman with green-pea eyes and hair made of bread tucked a baby boy into a bread-soup cradle. Moisés ate the little woman, carved out of a chicken breast, and Elias ate the cradle and the baby boy, carved from a chicken leg. That night, as the three of them went to sleep, the cook assumed a serious expression and said you're going to be a father. A smile slowly formed on Moisés's blank face. A smile formed on the cook's stern face. And not for a moment did they remember that they were more than seventy years old.

*A*s the just-arrived sheep greedily ripped into the grass with their teeth, filling the air with the sound of stubble being pulled and torn, I sat down under the big old cork tree. I stretched out my legs, and the sheepdog looked at me with a mournful gaze. A melancholy gaze that didn't last more than a fraction of an instant, a gaze that told me everything's going to end. A gaze that told me you'll go home to the farmstead, as we do every day, but the night will pass more slowly; you'll look over your shoulder at the last twists and turns of the thrushes in the sky and at that moment you'll want to be a thrush; your boots will feel heavier and the earth heavier, to dissuade you from going. A gaze that told me when it's time to drive the sheep back to the farmstead, you won't feel like getting up from under the cork tree, you'll feel like curling up and pretending that you don't exist and that the earth has swallowed you and that you're no longer responsible for anything. A gaze that told me it will be hard to cross the threshold of the door to your house, you'll look at the just-fallen night inviting you to be black, to blend with it, and to become perhaps a star.

IN THE MAIN HALLWAY OF THE RICH PEOPLE'S HOUSE, José's wife was sitting before the voice shut up in a chest and heard it say: perhaps the sky is a huge sea of fresh water and we, instead of walking under it, walk on top of it; perhaps we see everything upside down and the earth is a kind of sky, so that when we die, when we die, we fall and sink into the sky.

THE SHEEPDOG WANDERED OFF, like a sad thought. The sheep kept ripping at the deep-rooted stubble, and the baby lamb, which I usually carried under my arm, since it couldn't keep up with the others, suckled its grazing mother. The baby lamb, with a slender body, short and softer wool, and pretty, with a pretty voice, shrill like early mornings, busily sucking warm milk, its eyes closed. The sheep all shorn. Divided into gentle groups and folding over the contour of the land, they merged with it a little. In the time when my father was a shepherd and Doctor Mateus still cared about the farmstead and its affairs, the doctor thought that the sheep should be identified with his mark. I remember the men laughing or smiling as they branded the sheep amid a clamor of protests, baa-aa-aa-aa-aa, using a branding iron with the letter M inside a circle, an iron that they dipped in blue ink while saying who's next, who's next? They smiled and laughed, because the flock could never get mixed up with any other flock, since all the pastures to which they went belonged to Doctor Mateus, and all the lands and paths and roads on which they set foot belonged to Doctor Mateus; they smiled and laughed with the morning. These are the things that make up a man's life, I remember thinking. I thought this because I looked at the sky: the sky painted in the open spaces between the leaves of the cork tree, another plain above the plain, passing a little over the summit and falling behind it, the sky that held the sun and that wasn't just its light but managed, in its limpid visage, to be yet more light; the pure and serene sky, which I could say is infinitely pure, and serene enough to be dead, were it not for its over-whelming blood, its vast blood that's above us and before us and inside us, its undeniable and almost visible blood, forever ready to be our blood and to constitute our life, should we happen to look at it. I remember the sky on that day when the men laughed and smiled and branded the sheep. I looked at the sky. And now I remember the sky on that day when the sheep looked sad to my eyes, the sheep that once had no mark; the sky on that day so sad, because on that day I died a little more under the sky to which I nearly said farewell or to which I ridiculously did say farewell; the sky that looked at me with pity and without lying, enlightening me with what I once could have been, with what I am, wished to be, and won't ever be; the sky sincere like a sheepdog's gaze, like a mother's gaze, like a sky.

I didn't sleep during siesta. The dog's gaze spoke to me again, saying you will walk for a long time in silence.

ON THAT EXPIRING AUGUST EVENING, as he crossed the town under the night sky, the people sitting in their doorways greeted him with surprise in their voice, openly staring at him until he was out of sight. He reached the square wearing the black sheepskin on his back and with an old sack slung over his shoulder by a rope. His body still felt sore from the giant's kicks and from having been left all night on top of the stones and the protruding roots of the big old cork tree. There was mud on his boots. His trousers weren't their usual color but that of the sun's bleaching gaze. His chest was wrapped in the bonesetter's bandage. His shirt was drenched in sweat. He reached the square and his dog followed him. He entered Judas's general store: silence. On one side of the counter: the devil's smile. On the other side: the hunched giant, his head touching the ceiling. The men were scattered, hazy, mixed together, it being impossible to distinguish the beginning of one man from the end of another; men on all sides of the store, wide-eyed and waiting, amid the casks and the smell of wine. José didn't set down his staff, didn't set down his sack, didn't go up to the counter, didn't trace the veins in the marble with his finger. The giant walked up to José, with a veil made of the charcoal-drawn faces of all the men, and shoved him. In the square, swallowed by night, José stayed on his feet long enough for the giant to knock him down with a kick in the shins. At the door to the general store, the devil smiled in silence; the men, mixed up in an indefinite mass around the square, said nothing but were more silent than that; the giant couldn't be heard; José wasn't breathing or, if he was breathing, his breath couldn't be distinguished from the almost unbearable breeze of absolute silence. The giant's boots against José's prostrate body. The giant's boots against José's defenseless body. The giant's boots against the body without body of José without José. The whitewash of the houses surrounding the square was black with night. When the giant got tired, he went away. The devil vanished, smiling. The men slowly walked up to José. Eyes open. The stars. From the store Judas brought, between two fingers and with his

pinkie in the air, a glass of red wine that he poured on José's
parched lips. Many arms carried him, like a heavy sack or a
corpse, to the wagon of a man José didn't recognize. The bandage of the bonesetter still squeezed his chest. On the road to
the farmstead, crossing through the night as through a storm,
the sheepdog followed the wagon.

HE LET THE BABY LAMB RUN FREE on the ground and closed the
gate by coiling some rusty wires around a post. The sheep headed
for the trough that was filled with clean water from buckets or
for wherever else in the dusty pen they wanted to go. José walked
toward the house, just a few yards away. And that short distance
was so long and so slow. All his sorrow. All his sorrow that was
his wife and his believing in her, all his sorrows were packed into
that distance. José walked toward the house, and the thrushes, in
the gray sky, were not like flames in a fireplace, they were like a
forest fire with a gaping mouth swallowing branches and twigs,
dry leaves and the sky. The afternoon, dying, slowly entered into
José and into the heart of things: into the white walls of the rich
people's house, into the plains that were infinity on all sides, into
the shadow of the sheepdog's gaze. José walked and the afternoon absorbed him, and José walked over the afternoon. And
time became distorted, because the time José took to walk those
few yards was greater than the time that flowed in his veins or
the time of silence between heartbeats. It was a frozen time.
Frozen. With thrushes and other birds frozenly flying in the sky
that slid past them in an afternoon that refused to die. It was a
dead time of anxiety. So much time passed. And, after so much
time, José saw the house come toward him. It was finally night.
He stood before the door, and entered.

On the table the lamp's recently lit wick dispersed into the

air the weak but unmistakable smell of kerosene. Beneath that
steady light José's wife and their baby, whom she held in her lap,
poured long black shadows across the brick floor. With a spoon
for stirring coffee she fed him soup. She didn't look at José. The
child had a white dish towel tucked under his collar as a bib and
laughed at his father. José's overcast face was set in a quasi-idiotic
expression between laughing and crying. Indifferent because only
six months and two weeks old and because no one six months
and two weeks old understands the silence of a man weary of
anxiety, the boy looked at his father with baby eyes. José's arms
hung limp at his sides, hands open: José's thick and tired hands,
like two old people scorched by the sun, sitting in the sun with
their eyes closed, feeling only the sun and all the deaths they've
outlived, the faces that once were people sunken beneath the
earth and the distance of the night under the earth and the enormous distance of the earth on top of the lonely dead, the weight
of the earth in José's abandoned hands. His wife's eyes were of
black stone, perhaps basalt, and cold, and they traced perfectly
straight lines, resting sadly on the essential. Her hair was slightly
disheveled, and José felt like running his hand through the hair
of that lovely woman and saying sweet girl, saying sweet girl, he
felt like running his hand through her hair like a breeze, just the
palm of his gentle hand, and his fingers, his fingers, the tips of
his fingers through her hair, slowly penetrating, slowly passing
through her hair, and José saying sweet girl, saying sweet girl.
And, in José, the sad despair of having lost all certainties. A man
without certainties loses nearly all of what makes him a man. A
man without certainties is like a body without flesh, like ideas
without thought. A man emptied of certainties. An empty man.
Just the shell of a man before a woman he doesn't know, before
a son whom he doesn't know and who smiles at him. The boy's

hair was curly like José's. He ate spinach soup as well as bread soup, as if eating soup were important to him. He ate well. He smiled. José's wife, back curved, fed him soup without a mother's pride in her son's appetite. Indifferent. They poured long shadows, like black water, across the brick floor. Without setting down his staff or the sack slung over his shoulder by a rope, without removing the black sheepskin he wore on his back, without saying anything, he headed straight for the town.

WIFE. YOUR WHITE SKIN WAS A SUMMER I wished to live that was denied me. A path that didn't deceive me. What deceived me was the light and the bleary eyes of relived mornings. What deceived me was a dream of being the son I used to be, running all day through open country and measuring the wheat fields by the breadth of my open arms; I was deceived by a dream of being the son I used to be in the person of your husband and in your eyes, in your son, our own. Now I know that old mornings can't be relived. New days can't be built on top of remembered mornings. Perhaps I invented you, starting from a star like one of these. I wanted to have a star and to give it July mornings. Those glorious July mornings in front of our house while my mother finished making lunch, those tasty lunches, and my father arriving home and chiding her, but not seriously, for the lunch not being ready, and I sitting in the dirt, perhaps digging a hole, perhaps playing with my cardboard horse. I had a cardboard horse. I never told you, I told you very little, but I had a cardboard horse. I played with it and it was beautiful. I liked it a lot. A lot. Lots and lots. When my father brought it home, inside genuine wrapping paper, I anxiously started undoing the twine. When I saw it, with its little raised ears and shiny eyes, I stood still in front of it. It was my world for a week, can you believe it? That simple cardboard horse was my world for a week. But on Saturday I left it outside. My father called me for something, my mother called me for something, and I forgot it. Can you believe it? I forgot my cardboard horse in the backyard. How was it possible? How could I not remember it? How do people forget, like that, the things they cherish? I forgot my cardboard horse in the backyard. How could I sleep? How could I pull the covers over my breathing and sleep? How could I just sleep? I forgot my cardboard horse in the backyard, can you believe it? And that night it rained. On Sunday morning I woke up with lightning flashing in my eyes and thunder roaring in my chest: the cardboard horse? My cardboard horse? I ran to the backyard, racing through the kitchen in my underwear, I ran barefoot and, amid the puddles of clean water and the wet earth and drops of water hanging from the leaves of trees, I found the cardboard horse in the backyard where I'd left it. It was an amorphous pile of pulp in which I could make out two sad, glittering eyes, its washed-out colors painting the ground and the stones. I knelt before it and cried. That morning I cried. It was my father who pulled me away from there. For you, for our son, for me, I wanted a cardboard horse, without any rain. I wanted an impossible fantasy, without the blame that's inevitable. The blame that you and I didn't have. The fact that we exist guaranteeing condemnation. Like a precipice at the end of a race: the runners having to cross the finish line and that finish line being on the edge of a cliff. Or like a knife hanging over us, a knife that will sink into our back at any moment, for no reason, a knife we sometimes look at and we know that it's there ready to fall and that it will fall, at any moment, for no reason. A knife sunken in our back, to make us suffer or to make us die suffering. I didn't choose this fate. I chose roads suspecting that they were all the same. And they were all the same. I chose no roads, including this one. I didn't choose this night that makes me go back into town, that makes me go back to Judas's general store in search of the devil's false smile. This night that walks with my legs and that makes me, forces me, to go back to the giant. And you know very well that I don't want to; you know, even as you know your own name and other obvious things, you know I don't want and didn't choose this. It's true that I'm going. I walk and whoever sees me imagines it's my will. The way I'm walking is precisely my way of walking. I didn't choose this, don't want this, but I'm not going unwillingly. I know it's impossible not to go. It's impossible not to go. Impossible not to. Impossible. The sheepdog follows me, and between the grinding of my own slow steps I can hear the dog's quick, light paws. In the darkness the cicadas sketch the vastness of the plains with their song. I think: life is a punishment, a punishment with no sin or blame, a punishment without redemption; life is a punishment that nothing hinders and nothing authorizes. I imagine you watching this night from the balcony of my eyes and entering into this forest of a thousand uncounted stars, these stars that aren't enough to light up the earth but that light up tiny circumferences of sky surrounding them. I imagine you listening to me as perhaps you lull the baby to sleep with the lullabies that your father put you to sleep with when you were little and that he whistled in the brickyard in the afternoon.

Son. I wish there were a breeze that would explain to me your smile and another breeze that would explain to you, without hurting you, my silence. I wish I could learn the grin on your lips, the look of your eyes, and remind you of them when you're my age. I was your innocence once. And what it left me with was the huge innocence of believing. I believed I could give you a sky for you to play in and that life would be what we wanted. Just like that. Just by wanting, by trying hard, by working, we'd have what we longed for. I don't mean grandiose things, fancy clothes or horse-drawn carriages, but food, tasty and wholesome food, and a new cardboard horse, should you happen to forget yours in the backyard on a rainy night. I believed that the joy of your eyes and smile could return to your mother's and to my eyes, and remain intact in your own. I believed in so many things. I'm nearing the town, and I know what to expect: to die a little more. I'd rather you didn't know, but unfortunately not even this can I hide from you, because one day, when they tell you the story of your life, they'll tell you that on a starry night your father went into town and was beaten up; they'll tell you that a few days earlier he'd already been beaten up in the fields and that he kept on his path, with a bandage around his chest, knowing what to expect. They won't tell you that he thought about you while keeping on his path, and he told you secrets. They won't tell you, because they can't grasp this, that your father kept going for you, for you to have at least a sliver of what he dreamed of for you, for you to have some slight protection from what's stronger than you, always much stronger. They'll tell you that your father was beaten up, and beaten up again, and you'll be ashamed of me. The years will gradually erase everything I thought was sure but never was, until all that's left is what actually happened, and finally even that will be forgotten. The years will erase me, you'll see. And this doesn't make me sad, because I've always known that's how it would be. But I have to tell you this: I never wanted to desert you. If I did so, it was against my will. Beautiful, tiny son, happy and free. I've just entered the town. The people look at me, uttering drawled good evenings. I know you're too young to understand everything I want to tell you, but from all of this I'd like you to remember at least the word father, at least the word father.

I'd like you to look me in the eye, even when I'm long gone and share with the earth its solitude; I'd like you to learn and discover what I thought for you on this night. I'm in the square. I'm in the general store. On one side of the counter: the devil's smile. On the other side: the hunched giant, his head touching the ceiling.

$\mathcal{Y}$ESTERDAY I HEARD A WAGON go by in the middle of the night, and I looked out my bedroom window. It was Paulo's son, and he was hauling José. I put on boots and went outside, in my undershirt and long johns, to see in what state he'd been left this time. His eyes were wide open, as when I brought him from the fields in a wheelbarrow, and his body was beaten to a pulp. There was no blood on his face. I told Paulo's son to keep going and sent my greetings to his father. I looked out my bedroom window, I saw the wagon reach José's house and his wife open the door before anyone knocked. She didn't seem shocked or upset. She didn't speak. She grabbed under the arms, Paulo's son grabbed the legs, and they carried

José's body into the house. The wagon headed back into town, its squeaky iron wheels occasionally making sparks against the stones and the mules walking faster than their age. José's wife came to shut the door, and although my lights were out, she looked at me, as if she could see through the dark or had the eyes of a cat. She shut the door.

Today, when I arrived at the house of Moisés, Elias, and the cook, they were all still in bed. I knocked on the door, I called, I knocked, and I sat down on the stone bench outside the house of the man shut up in a room writing. A young man passed by who seemed to be about forty years old and whom I didn't know, for I've lost track of those who are born and die or move away, of the children and grandchildren of this or that person, and of the great-grandchildren and great-great-grandchildren of this or that person whom I did know, yes, with them I spun many tops and gleaned many olives. A young man passed by whom I didn't have the patience to ask whose son are you?, whom I didn't have the patience to ask whose grandson are you?, whom I didn't have the patience to ask whose great-grandson are you? A young man passed by who greeted me very politely and told me, in almost a whisper, to tell José not to come back into town anytime soon, because the devil meant to do him more harm, because the devil had a grudge against him and meant to do him more harm. I didn't ask the young man how he knew this, I merely said yes, I'd give him the message. The young man was passing by the fountain's weak trickle when I heard the lock turn in the door to the brothers' house. It was the bleary-eyed cook. I handed her a sack of late-season peas and went in. The brothers were drinking coffee and eating some odd-looking biscuits, shaped like pacifiers. The thin white hair of both Elias and Moisés was uncombed, and it was the latter who told me the kid won't let us sleep. Elias whispered into his brother's ear and Moisés turned to me and repeated she doesn't sleep at night, but if you look at her now, she's sleeping like a princess. And indeed she was. The cook's house wasn't very big. The largest room was the kitchen; it had a fireplace with a fire that was always lit and surrounded by pots, a washbasin, a table, and a sink, and the walls were covered with all sorts of enamel, aluminum, and even copper pots and pans. A door in the kitchen led to the backyard, where Moisés kept a cabbage patch that was always luxuriant, thanks to all the manure it received, for it was in the backyard that they did their necessities. The bedroom was small for the size of the bed where they all slept, and even smaller with the little crib wedged between the bed and the wardrobe. One of the bedroom walls abutted the house of the man who writes in a room without windows, and Moisés told me that at night, when the baby forgot to cry or she paused to regain her strength, they could hear the fountain pen tracing letters on paper, they could hear their neighbor crumpling page after page, and they could sometimes even hear him dip his pen ever so softly in the inkwell. I cracked open the bedroom door and it was just like Moisés had said. The girl, uncovered, contentedly slept like a grown-up. Her large and very round cheeks whistled a cadenced sigh, her full-fleshed tummy bulged out of her diaper, and her legs, full of folds, were spread apart in leisurely abandon. I gently closed the door and turned back to the brothers' haggard faces. The cook was cooking. Moisés explained that he was very fond of his baby girl and that when he looked at her it was as if he were looking at a sun, but he hadn't had a good night's rest since she was born three months ago. Elias, nodding his head slowly, concurred. The eyes of both brothers had become smaller, being surrounded by black rims and sunken into their sockets, as if dropped to the bottom of a well. When the cook was pregnant, everyone thought she was carrying twins that would perhaps also be stuck together. Everyone thought this because the cook's belly was bigger than two pregnant bellies, and on the day when her nine months burst, there was room in there for a three-year-old or, if the suspicions were confirmed, for two children aged one and a half. In spite of her unprecedented belly, she never stopped cooking and making treats to satisfy her cravings: floating cream puffs with sardines, pigeons stuffed with sponge cake, gelatin with pork testicles. Halfway through winter, when the cook was seven months pregnant, they were all sleeping when a muffled cry reverberated throughout the bedroom and woke them up. They realized it had come from the cook's belly, her belly that was a mountain covered by blankets. And the cook said it already has a voice, and, taking her belly in her arms, she began singing a lullaby interspersed with yawns until the unborn creature quieted and fell asleep. On the day when the cook's water broke and she began panting like a fox under a hot sun, the brothers went to notify the midwife, who in turn notified her brother, who had a carpenter's bench and made coffins. She's no doubt carrying twins, and as old as she is she's sure not to make it, said the midwife in a low voice, convinced of the failure she considered self-evident. The delivery lasted more than twelve hours, and as the morning wore on people began gathering at the front door of the house where the cook and the brothers lived. After lunch the crowd reached the door of the house of the man shut up in a room writing. After supper the crowd reached as far as the fountain at the end of the street. The midwife marveled at the hardiness of the cook, who did almost everything by herself. Nearly all of the townspeople were in the street commenting and making bets, when Moisés came to the door struggling with the weight of the baby girl in his arms. Rosy-cheeked, she weighed twenty-four pounds, and never had the town seen such a chubby baby. She was born with her eyes open, astonished at the world. Everyone on the street clapped their hands, cheered and hoorayed, and they carried the baby, the midwife, Moisés, and Elias in the air. They threw a dance, which didn't last into the early morning only because the next day was a workday. The cook, very sore, slept in the bedroom.

YESTERDAY, WHEN THE WAGON ARRIVED with José, I already had the tub ready and water on the fire. I helped get him off the wagon. I was somewhat surprised that he had no blood on his face. The man who brought him handed me José's lunch sack and shepherd's staff and left. Old Gabriel watched us from his window. Despite his hundred and some years of age, he still sticks his nose in other people's business. I stripped José, without removing the bonesetter's bandage, and accommodated him as best I could in the tub. He couldn't hold his neck up, his arms and legs drooped to the ground, his body adopted the shape of the tub, and only his eyes conserved a flicker of light or of life. The water was lukewarm, just the right temperature, and I poured the pans onto his chest: thick jets of water, small rivers of lukewarm water curving in the air and falling over his body, streams, lakes, reservoirs. I washed him, and his skin: I filled the palms of my hands with water and spread it over his chest, on his back; I rubbed soap over his legs, his shoulders, and my fingertips glided over the contours of his skin. I washed him, and his body: I passed the towel over his face, redrawing the lines of his face, more relaxed, serene; I wrapped him up in the towel, or maybe I hugged him, for I felt him inside my arms, next to my breasts. I tucked him in bed, and if his eyes hadn't remained wide open

67

in a fixed trance, he would have felt comfortable. The baby slept soundly. I slept soundly.

This morning I did my housework while he, immobile, remained in a deep insomnia or a deep sleep. I took care of the baby, who played a little and then got drowsy again, so I put him to bed. The tub was still next to the fireplace and I remembered the bath I took a month after the baby was born. It was the first time I'd had my period since getting pregnant, and it was on the last day, the amount of blood on the rags diminishing, diminishing until it was almost nothing, and at sundown I felt like taking a bath. I filled the tub and, standing up in it, threw water over myself. Hot water that felt cold anyway, clean water making me clean. On that day the baby was sleeping. I couldn't resist and sat down. I let my arms and legs and hair hang outside the tub, closed my eyes and sat there. Thousands of armies in my body finally rested, I was out of breath in my bliss. Naked, I glowed in a honey light that passed through the curtains. In my body men knocked off work and put down their hoes, mules went home and tasted their first handful of grass after pulling wagons all day, and the turned earth finally found its order in the repose of night. My filth and my blood's ardor slowly dissolved in the water. And slowly I was.

CATCHING A PAUSE IN THE BROTHERS' GAZING, I told them what had happened to José the night before. They stared ahead and held their peace, and it was the cook who, overcoming her resentment at some ambiguous flirtations for which she'd stopped talking to me over twenty years ago, it was the cook who turned around from the stove and said José was always a good man, if he had time at night he would talk with me in the garden of the rich people's house, if he found herbs in the fields he would bring them to me in the kitchen and I'd throw cumin, thyme, pennyroyal, mountain parsley, I'd throw everything onto the steaks and stewed lamb, but that girl he got married to, that girl he got married to . . . And her voice trailed off into unintelligible murmurs. I was astonished by the cook's voice, she had greatly aged.

The oil press is close by and I went there with the brothers to see if all was in order. What we said going and coming was of no importance and I've already forgotten it. When we returned, lunch was ready to serve and we sat down. What we ate was a faithful replica of the town, in miniature and seen from the sky: the central square, the streets, and the white houses, all in the smallest detail. The earth and the paving stones were molded out of pork slices, the dust of the earth was pepper, the houses were mashed potatoes, the rooftops were red peppers, and there was even smoke or steam issuing from the houses' chimneys. I also got to see the little girl awake and eating lunch. The cook had made her an enormous baby-food bear that looked like it was plush. First she ate its legs, then she ate its arms, then its trunk, then the head, and then she burped.

Before leaving town, I went to see José's father. In his daughter's backyard, José's dead father was sitting in front of the chicken coop, alive. I knew he was alive, because his chest moved slowly in and out, bound to a respiration that was no longer his, since he'd abandoned his a long time ago, a time that must have seemed to him like years, for José's father is a dead man, frozen in eternity, and in eternity, with no beginning or end, a second is eternal, and the time spent in eternity is a succession of eternities. I sat down next to him and realized, from his gaze obliviously fixed on a point he didn't see, that he was dead. No one can do you any more harm. Where you are, silence is an agony. And you never fled from suffering, as you never fled from life. Mourning weighs heavy on us, friend, but whoever flees from it will be its worst victim. We both know this. You can no longer rest, the invincible depths of death have sucked you into its infinite interior. You're falling, sucked down, in that longest of descents. Your body, your drooping arms, your open hands, your uncertain legs, your hunched back, your aimless gaze, and your frightened face are in this backyard, next to me, but you aren't here, dear friend. You were once strong, and today you're much stronger, for you've crossed through the gates of death and entered its garden of despair, and you're where blackness doesn't end in a new day. You're on the path that can only be traveled alone and at night, for we all have a gate and a garden to cross into, alone, at night, beneath and above and amid fear. You're dead and, inside death, you know you're dead. We both know. All that you imagined in the word hope has lost its meaning. There is no hope, for we're too small, we amount to very little. We're a pine needle before a fire, we're a speck of dirt before an earthquake, we're a drop of dew before a storm, dear friend. The world, indifferent to the world that contained José's father and that José's father contained in himself, went on. The chicks emitted a light rain of mournful peeps, the chickens clucked with indignation, the rooster occasionally squawked. Even in the shade the sun seethed and burned. In the enclosed area behind the backyard wall, the sun raised a sweltering mist of the leavings from a small wheat field. And without talking, since words are the worst way of saying something, I looked at José's father, knowing he couldn't hear me, and said your son is in a bad way, your son is suffering. And I said no more. Not because I had no more to say but because there was no way to say it, not even without words. There's no way to explain all that we're saying when we say suffering.

THE AFTERNOON IS WANING. I can finally let in a little light through the windows, rescuing the house from the shadows. José looks the same. I covered him with a sheet, I propped him up with two pillows, as if he were sitting before getting out of bed, and he looks the same, eyes wide open, wanting to swallow the world with his gaze. The baby is peacefully playing with a wooden spoon on the quilt I spread on the kitchen floor. I wish I could be so peaceful. The afternoon isn't waning in me. In me the day seethes and evening won't arrive. All my days are sure to seethe. All my days will seethe until I cease, and afterward; all my days will be August and the hot season; all my days will forever be the summer roasting me like a torturer with red-hot irons. That much I'm sure of. I leave the door open, to keep an eye on the baby, and go into the little garden. I fill the watering can and sprinkle the flowers. How I'd love to be a mallow and be watered. How I'd love to be a mallow and endure the hottest hour knowing I'd have water like this, so cool and real, dripping down my leaves and throat, soaking my roots and hair. The afternoon is waning. Soon I'll see old Gabriel coming up the slope to the house. The afternoon is waning. The plain is old from having seen so much. It knows the life of the birds, which it releases as messengers into the sky; it knows the life of the cicadas, which it shelters in its skin so that they can sing after the heat has passed; it knows the life of people, which it allows and mercifully buries. The cork trees in the distance bow toward the earth as much as possible, wanting the coolness they feel in their roots all over their trunks, all through their sap, in their highest branches; they bow toward the earth as if condemned, bewailing the sun that singes their cork, just as it does a child's soft skin. I place my fingers under the water that comes out of the zinc can's tiny holes.

I see old Gabriel, coming up the slope to the house. Good afternoon, he says. I reply by looking at him. He enters the house through the open door without asking permission, since, José being here, he never asks permission. The baby holds still while looking at him, and Gabriel remains still while looking at the baby. An old man more than a hundred years old and a child who knows nothing about the world. An old man who knows everything about the world and a six-month-old child. I set down the watering can. I start walking toward the bedroom window. Still at some distance, I can see that the old man has sat down in the wicker chair. I walk closer to the bedroom window. I lean against the wall and make not even the sound of breathing. The two men are silent. Standing next to the wall, I look at the rich people's house across the way and listen at the window, which I'd cracked open to let in some air so that it would clear José's mind of idle musings, and I can hear that they are silent. The pigeons stop fluttering around the eaves of the rich people's house and stare at me, leaning against the wall. Old Gabriel breaks the silence of a multitude that shouts the end of afternoon, he adds his own words to it, saying don't go back into town anytime soon, don't go, I've heard that the devil means to do you more harm, I've heard he has a grudge against you and means to do you more harm; if you have any respect or consideration for me, don't go back into town; for your miserable father's sake, for your mother who so loved you, for your son in the next room, don't go back into town; wait a month or two, I beg you, but don't go back into town anytime soon.

I WALK ON THE ROAD, surrounded by the plain, and I think of José's father, surrounded by death. The nocturnal plain of death. Nocturnal, even if all of this is the day, all of this indefinite light that defines things. This plain. And all this land that makes me wish I were big enough to lie down on top of it and cover it all. All of this plain that transcends time. This profoundly sad plain, buried in its own eternity. The wagons with the field workers pass by. They're tired and carry a bit of this plain in their faces. They look at me and rob a little strength from their bodies to greet me while they pass by. I, appreciative, greet them in return. Tomorrow, very early in the morning, they'll make this trip again, and they'll make it so many times, so many times, that one day they won't know if to return means to return home, at day's end, or if it means to return to the fields, at dawn. To where I'm going, to wherever I go, the plain goes with me. The cork trees and the holm oaks vanish behind me and are replaced by cork trees and holm oaks. I see wrinkly young corks growing which, a few yards later, turn into tall and broad cork trees. I walk and am nearing the farmstead. I've reached the slope. I feel the road's many stones under my feet. I feel their oldness under my feet. José's wife is watering the little garden that the rich woman likes to see kept up. Good afternoon. The door to José's house is open and I enter. His son, sitting against a pillow on a quilt, holds a wooden spoon in his hand. He looks at me with more intensity than a baby is capable of. He'll soon be a man. In the bedroom, José's wide-eyed gaze is that of an orphan in the moment when he becomes an orphan. I sit down in front of him. I look at him trying to see inside him, but there's a barrier that won't let me, a black wall, like a tightly drawn curtain of night. Outside José's wife has leaned against the wall. I know this not because I see her or hear the slightest movement but because I feel her through the wall and because I hear the faint sound of her listening, for there's no action that doesn't have a sound, and that sound can be identified if we're sufficiently attentive and have lived long enough to know these things. José just lies there. I hope he can hear and understand my words. I tell him don't go back into town anytime soon, don't go, I've heard that the devil means to do you more harm, I've heard he has a grudge against you and means to do you more harm; if you have any respect or consideration for me, don't go back into town; for your miserable father's sake, for your mother who so loved you, for your son in the next room, don't go back into town; wait a month or two, I beg you, but don't go back into town anytime soon.

EOPLE ARE A SMALL PART OF the world, and I don't understand people. I know what they do and the immediate motives for what they do, but to know this is to know what's plain to see, it's to know nothing at all. I think: perhaps people are, perhaps they exist, with no explanation for it; perhaps people are pieces of chaos on top of the disorder they enclose, and perhaps this explains them. There was a sun inside of a sun inside of a sun in my gaze, but I know that today, beyond me and beyond the utterly nocturnal light that I've become, a night went by, out there in the sky, out there in the room where I lie. I know that my wife and son slept soundly. I was tortured by monsters molded in the darkness out of the sun that blinds me, with huge feet and huge claws that ripped at what I am, while they slept soundly. It's better this way. Better that I suffer and am defeated, letting nothing touch your gazes, which I've always sought to protect. I've always sought to protect you from what destroys slowly instead of killing at once. I've always sought to defend you, and even in that I was defeated, I was defeated in everything, for I know that, sooner or later, your faces will also know suffering; sooner or later you too, dear wife whom I loved more than anything, will die, and you, my dear son, will die. For a while our tombstones in the cemetery will be cared for and visited by those we left behind, but they too will die one day, and our tombstones will be overrun by moss and grass, and the people who pass by us won't stop, and even those we left behind won't be remembered by anyone, because everything they loved will have died; and that house that was important to us will have disappeared, perhaps a cork tree will grow up in its stead, and the cemetery where we were buried will be razed, and someone we never knew will plow the land into which we were transformed, and that someone who won't remember us will plow the land thinking perhaps of his children and dreaming of the future and forgetting that he too will die and become earth, as well as his small children and his children's children. I know that a morning or an afternoon or a day came and went and that old Gabriel came to see me. He said words that to me were indistinguishable from music, the music of harps, and I discovered that old Gabriel isn't a man. No man could resist more than a hundred years without his body getting tired or his enthusiasm for life running out. I envy him. I remember being little and seeing him in the garden, raising his hoe and driving it into the earth with all his might; I remember everything he taught me, and how together we'd steal birds from their nests, as if we were the same age but always knowing that we weren't; I remember the great respect he showed for me and that I showed him in return, never out of obligation. Today I respect you even more, and I know that my son will also learn from you, I know that my son will also discover with you the smell of turned earth, the sound of the hoe digging into the ground. And there can be no sadness in that. He said words I couldn't decipher, because they were transformed into music as they left his mouth. A music like I've never heard, a music of instruments I don't recognize but presume to be harps, since harps are the instruments of angels. He said words I couldn't decipher, because they weren't to be deciphered, even if old Gabriel's gaze tried its best. And the night returned. No doubt about that. The night always returns.

A NIGHT WENT BY. The morning dawned across the plain and on the roof of the rich people's house, and José got out of bed as if it were just another morning after having slept a good night's sleep. His wife also woke up. She began to get dressed and didn't lift her eyes off the floor, not even when José stopped to stare at her, throwing everything else in his gaze out of focus. José went outside and took a deep breath. It was a fine morning for coming back to life. Although it was still early, the first heat could already be felt in a very soft breeze, or in the passage of José's skin through the air. He walked around the waterwheel. He went up to the washtub and, seeing that it was full of clean water, he dipped in his hands, looking at them for a long time as if waiting for them to release something, as if they were covered with blood and the blood would slowly break loose; he lowered his face to the tub and, on an impulse, lifted his cupped hands and doused his face with water: once, twice. The water ran down his face, and he didn't feel the coolness he'd expected, he didn't feel himself wake up or be born. He couldn't fool his weariness with the cool, clean water. By then the sheepdog was already at his heels. And José and the dog slowly walked to the gates that shut up the flock. All the sheep were lying under the roof. There were about two hundred sheep lying under a roof that didn't even protect them from the wind, rain, or sun; two hundred sheep under a few rows of roof tiles supported by old joists, roof tiles held up in the air by pinewood posts made shiny by the friction of the sheep's wool and imbued with their smell. In the feed troughs there were still vestiges of the armfuls of hay that old Gabriel had placed there the night before. The sheepdog pushed against the gate that José opened by undoing a tangle of wires. The dog ran in and drove the sheep out with barks that sounded very different from when she was young, with monotonous barks that nonetheless made the sheep react and crowd around the gate in their haste to get out. Supporting most of his weight on his staff, José slowly followed behind the sheep. The dog, working endlessly, ran around the flock to keep it together and to make it wait for the shepherd. José was the shadow of a man who was very tired and far away from that landscape, or very close and inside the plain and the infant sun; he was the shadow of a man with a staff in his hand and, on his back, the black hide of a sheep that he had raised and that he always remembered when he wore its hide like a coat, but not because the sheep was different from others. He was the shadow of a man in the morning, with a sack slung over his shoulder by a rope and with a baby lamb under his arm.

Unbeknownst to José, at that moment his name was being whispered in one of the bedrooms in town. The baby daughter of Moisés and the cook had just fallen asleep. After pulling her slip over her breast, flaccid and sticky from the baby's mouth, the cook got under the sheets, turned her face to Moisés, and said today you're going to the Mount of Olives, you must go there before the sun sets and give José a message from me. Take him a pot of stewed lamb and tell him not to come back into town anytime soon. If he asks you why, say that I was the one who sent you with this message. Moisés, having no desire to go, lay there for a few moments resigning himself to the idea and closed his eyes.

MY BROTHER HAS BEEN UNBEARABLE. He's forever complaining about the cook and the baby, as if the cook were to blame for the baby being awake at night and asleep during the day, and as if the baby were to blame for being three months old. Today, when I told him that I wanted us to finish up early at the oil press so that we could go to the Mount of Olives, he leaned into my ear and whispered, in a huff, I'm not going, I can tell you right now that I'm not going, I'm not about to go all the way out there under the hot sun to do nothing. We remained cross with each other until we sat down for lunch. The cook had made two twin brothers just like us, and a cook just like her, with a very fat baby girl in her lap. It looked like a portrait, so true to life were the features of the figures, and so true to life was their look of contentment. At that point my brother leaned over to me and said if you want to go to the Mount of Olives, we can go. The figures, posing in a row across the platter, were made of a homogeneous mass whose ingredients I couldn't identify. They tasted like fish, perhaps bass, perhaps boce, perhaps carp.

As soon as the last house in town was behind us, sweat did indeed begin to soak our skin all over, under our caps, under our arms, under our long johns. At the bend by the bog the pot already weighed heavy in my arm, but I kept quiet and didn't ask my brother to relieve me. On a piece of land belonging to Doctor

Mateus, the men were stripping off cork next to the road. We stopped for a moment, and the women who carried around water came over and offered us some in a cork bowl. Thanking them through my mouth, my brother accepted. I declined. And although I tried to focus on the men in the trees stripping away cork with axes, although I tried to focus on the men tossing slabs of cork as tall as they were on top of a stack in a wagon, all I could see were the women leisurely uncorking the jug, pouring cool water into the bowl, my brother slowly drinking it, the sound of the water slowly going down his throat, and my brother asking for another bowl, the women smiling, leisurely uncorking the jug, pouring cool water into the bowl, my brother slowly drinking it, and the sound of the water slowly going down his throat. We continued on our way, and the stewed lamb sloshing about in the pot got heavier. My brother was refreshed, and I tried to regain my strength in the occasional stretches of shaded road.

We reached the fence around the farmstead, and I forgot all my previous exertion, concentrating only on climbing the slope, which isn't even very steep or very long, and I think: we're almost there. We still haven't climbed a quarter of the slope. The sun beats down with all its unlimited might. I've climbed a quarter of the slope and think: we're almost there. We have to climb three times more than this stretch that was exhausting. Three times the time it took us so far. I think we're almost there, and I think of the cook telling me go to the Mount of Olives, go and deliver this message. I think of her gaze. And we reach the top of the slope. We knock on José's door. We greet his wife. She doesn't answer us or look at us. We ask for José. She slowly shakes her head, as if considering whether she really has to respond, and then says with a minimum of words and in a muffled voice, her hand in front of her mouth, that he's out in the fields. We thank her. She closes the door. We sit down on a white-washed stone bench in the shade, in front of the rich people's house, and wait.

I'VE BEEN KEEPING SHEEP FOR YEARS and not one of them has ever looked straight at me. My wife. She looked straight at me one day. That afternoon, a little over a year ago, we made our son, and I thought that that's how all people come together. A person arrives out of nowhere, for no special reason or for a reason that's unclear, and offers himself or herself to someone else, who finds it perfectly natural, since that's how all people come together, and in that great moment they both give themselves to each other for life, without looking back or thinking twice, they both give themselves to each other for life, since from that great moment on, the rest of life will be equally natural, inexplicable, and grand. What I didn't know is that what in one moment is the whole world won't always be the whole world. Before I got married everyone called her slut. So how's the slut doing? Everyone called her whore. So how's the whore doing? After I got married, they stopped calling her slut or whore. So how's your wife doing? And they thought slut, they thought whore. We got married and my wife never again left the farmstead. I don't know her smile, and I've often imagined how it would be, but I lost all hope of seeing it a long time ago. I don't know the touch of her hands, perhaps soft, perhaps rough, and I've often imagined how it would be. I don't know happiness in her, however furtive or fleeting, and I lost all hope of seeing her happy a long time ago. I don't know what destroyed us. We're ruins. We're what once was a house with living people and growing children, smoke in the chimney and open windows on summer nights, and today is a heap of bricks eroded by the rain, broken roof tiles on the ground, rubble and dirt strewn across the rotted floor, and grass growing between the floorboards. Were we ever anything solid, a real household? For me, yes. For my wife, I don't know. I've never known how she feels about anything.

Although it doesn't matter to me now, I know it's time to go back home. The sheepdog tells me so with her eyes, impatiently circling around me. I shout out a syllable that doesn't seem like it's from me. She rounds up the flock. We walk to the homestead. The flock is a river that, tripping over all the stones, flows with difficulty, and it is tempered by a flow greater than its own. The field is a member of the family. We've talked many times. He tells me things. And I've confessed things to him that I've never told anyone. He has protected and lulled and comforted me. The evening is slowly settling over the field. The sun is getting weaker. I tie around the gatepost the wires that enclose the sheep. I see the brothers rise from the bench where the old housekeeper used to sit while watching the rich people's children play. They walk up to me.

MOISÉS WALKED UP TO JOSÉ. He said nothing of what he knew about the drubbings from the giant, nor did he ask about them, nor did he mention anything that could lead to that subject. He handed him the pot of food and greeted him as usual, but he looked at him differently. José's wife came outside to empty a tub, flinging the water a considerable distance, then went to water the little garden next to the waterwheel. José glued his eyes on her immediately. Moisés said something unimportant that he had no real interest in saying, like haven't seen you for a while, or I have a little girl who's the cutest thing but doesn't let me sleep, or the cook often remembers being here at the farmstead; he said something unimportant and asked something unimportant, like how's your father doing?, or how's your little boy doing?, or how are you doing? José didn't answer, because he didn't hear. He was watching his wife, every one of his wife's movements, with a serious expression. Elias said something into his brother's ear to hurry him up, because he hoped they could catch a ride from one of the wagons that take workers to and from the fields. Moisés stopped dallying and said don't go back into town anytime soon. There was no change in José's expression. Moisés repeated don't go back into town anytime soon, it's the cook who sent me here to tell you this. José held his gaze and didn't hear a single word spoken by Moisés. The brothers said goodbye and left. Until the day became pure night, José remained in the middle of the courtyard, impassively watching his wife, every one of his wife's movements.

WE WEREN'T IN TIME TO catch a ride with the last wagon and we returned to town on foot. Before we'd gone a third of the way, night had fallen. Then the heat wasn't so bad, but we've grown old. My brother has felt a bit put out by my little girl, and I understand; he feels put out by the cook and complains to me, and I understand. I understand, because I know how it is. As surely as I'm standing here, he likes the girl no less than I, who am her father, and he has secretly liked the cook since the day we met her at José's wedding. I can see it. If we're alone with the girl, he passes his hand over her face and says coochie-coochie-coo. He plays with her hair. She, intrigued at how we look alike, stares at him with all the attention that a three-month-old can muster, and he, checking to make sure we're really alone, says coochie-coochie-coo. He doesn't say anything to the cook, but I see the way he looks at her each time she presents one of her artistic meals. He looks at her with respect, as if congratulating her. I realize it's hard for him to see the rent money from our house swallowed up month after month by her fancy dishes, but if my brother sometimes remembers this and complains into my ear, I'm sure that he forgets about it more often than not and simply delights in her lunches. And on our way back to town I repeated it to myself and said we've grown old. Our legs used to walk this road four or five times a day, back and forth, they walked this road without feeling even half as tired. If we were in a hurry, and young men are always in a hurry to get somewhere and to go from there to somewhere else, and from there to somewhere else; if we were in a hurry, we'd break into a run, and when we reached the town we were fresh as daisies, as if we'd been sitting there gabbing all afternoon. Now our weight weighs heavy on our legs. We watch where we place our feet, careful not to fall, for if we broke a leg it would be our death. We feel an invisible shaking in our legs, and lately that shaking has doubled and is noticeable in our gaze. Our bones don't bend the way they used to. Even our breathing is different from what it was. It used to be continuous, it was something we didn't notice. Now it takes more effort to breathe in, and when we breathe out we make an asthmatic sound, as if our throats were partly obstructed or we'd swallowed a rusty harmonica. Dead tired, we reached the town and our house. The baby was sleeping. She won't sleep a wink during the night, said my brother. The cook helped us take off our boots and unbend our toes. Since the baby's schedule was topsy-turvy, ours was too, and in spite of it being still early we had dinner. We sat down and the cook asked me does this day remind you of anything special? I stopped to think and couldn't remember anything special. My brother whispered into my ear that maybe it was our one-year wedding anniversary. Indeed it was. Smiling like a teenager, the cook presented a dish just for me that was an infinite spiral in the shape of a heart. It was made of mushrooms that my brother had picked and with strips of sirloin that must, on their own, have cost almost a month's rent. It was flavored with such an extravagant blend of spices that I couldn't identify a single one. It was one of the tastiest meals I've ever eaten. I ate the whole thing. I wiped my mouth on the back of my hand, and the cook slipped around me and whispered I love you. I smiled. Although I was exhausted and in spite of the baby waking up every fifteen minutes, that night we made love more than once.

EARLY IN THE MORNING Moisés went into the backyard. He squatted next to a cabbage and began to defecate. He laboriously wiped himself clean and got up. His sleepy brother waited and then asked do you have a stomachache? They went back to bed, and on the way to the oil press, they made no mention of what had happened. Moisés, if possible, felt even more worn out than the day before. The discomfort of being enervated only torments the flesh after a night of sleep, and that was how Elias explained the weariness that his brother felt in his limbs. The eaves of the houses still cast a shadow, and the brothers, bent forward, walked under this strip of shelter. They walked without seeing the streets. No one had taken notice, but since Moisés had gotten married, the brothers always walked to the door of their old house, from where they turned and followed the path they'd always taken to the oil press. It was useless to go by way of their old house, which lay in the wrong direction, but that's what they did. They did it not out of superstition but out of habit. And this time the whitewashed houses were so sad as they desperately tried in vain to talk to the brothers. It was as if they wished to catch their attention at all costs. It was as if they wished to say goodbye to the brothers and already missed them. The white-washed houses that the brothers passed every day. Bonds are formed between eternal things, and the brothers passing by those houses every day was as eternal as the white lime coating their walls. The houses' memory had gotten used to the brothers' slow passing, as it had gotten used to the sky and used to the sun. The accumulated moments of when the brothers passed by, on that unchanging path before each house, added up to a lot of time, even in the life of a house. And tears of white light ran down the walls as the brothers passed by.

Before the gate of the oil press, they both straightened up as much as they could, but it was Moisés who took the key from his pocket and inserted it into the lock. Then another lock. The ca-denced voice of a lament dripped from the oil tanks like the cry of a mother weeping for a child, a cry of black despair, embodied in the sound of the oil drops. Blackness was what Moisés and Elias felt. As if they had entered a tunnel, they perceived deep within, ever deeper, that something was approaching that would separate them. They could read, deep down, that this moment stood waiting for them in the future and that time was burning, going up in smoke before their eyes. At the same time and with the same images, and with the same words, the brothers remem-bered what they were leaving behind: the little girl, the cook, the face of their father etched in their memory, what they had heard and imagined about their mother. They remembered the little girl waking up at night and falling back asleep in their four inter-twined arms; the girl closing her eyes and truly knowing, more than she'd ever know if she were grown up, that they loved her. The cook, sitting by the fire and watching them eat, more gratified than if she herself were eating; happy, the way a man wishes the woman he loves to be happy. Their father, who taught them half of life and who died with his eyes fixed on them, as if he had nothing but them and was proud of what he had achieved. And their mother, whom they'd never even seen in a picture but whom they both could see in their minds: very young, with curly hair and large brown eyes. Everything that they were leaving behind, the mornings when the sun was mild, the path to the oil press; it all crowded into their memory, for the thing that would separate them was approaching: much worse than the man who pulls teeth with pliers, worse than a whetted knife separating them, worse than scissors. The morning was rising over the streets of the town and the plains that surrounded it, but in the oil press a still silence grew darker.

They sat there without speaking. Each looked in a different direction, at nothing. Behind their sad faces, they pondered. In his mind Moisés said words to his brother, hoping they'd be heard; in his mind he said it will be an instant and bring solitude. For the first time we'll shout each other's name. We've never needed to call each other by name, have you noticed? I don't know how my name sounds in your voice. In your voice, brother. Brother. I don't know how your name sounds in my voice. For the first time we'll shout each other's name, and our despair will be the prelude to a painful sorrow that we'll get used to, as a man without a heart gets used to the black void in his chest. You've always lived in my life, and I've always been with you when you smiled. Today we'll know solitude. We'll vanish from each other's life. But we won't forget. And to remember will be the greatest suffering, to remember what we were wherever we end up and not to be able to be anything anymore. To remember speaking in the way that only we spoke and to remain with that language in our heads, that way of speaking which we'll never use with anyone else. Today I'll leave you, knowing that I've always loved you for you having always been with me. And I'm no longer ashamed of that word we never said, love, that word, love, which we never once said but which today I need to say. Sincere, true, brother. I'll miss you. With no one to explain it to, since I'll have no one at my side, I'll miss you. And however black the plain may be where I'll roam for eternity, it will always be the painful memory of a sunset, it will always be the grief of only being able to remember you.

And with a sudden light that made his insides flare, Moisés's bowels ignited in a rampant fire, kindled by an overwhelming asphyxia, a fire and a light that burned holes in his belly, that hammered nails into his belly, that slashed his belly like an ax; in Moisés's belly a thousand armies walked barefoot over live coals, a thousand armadas ripped with razor-sharp rudders through fiery tides; Moisés's belly was light and fire, light and fire, a sudden sun born with the intensity of midday, the blaze from a match fallen on oil poured over his guts. Moisés was bent over his stomach, and Elias was bent over his stomach. Both brothers felt the same hell burning the inside of their skin. The walls of the oil press shouted a chorus of screams that, to the brothers' hearing, were a single scream scraping the inside of their ears with a pointy firebrand, and the brothers imagined that the voice sounded throughout the world: that the water flowing in brooks was that shrillness, and that the silence of birds and crickets on the plains had been replaced by that deafening intensity which was toppling trees, uprooting houses and stones, and driving people mad with the voracity of a cyclone. Moisés was burning up inside, and Elias felt the same flames. But they both knew it was Moisés who was dying. Moisés fell to his knees, Elias fell to his knees. And in the bowels of both brothers a bloody-eyed witch stirred a cauldron of flames and embers, a river overflowed its banks and flooded the fields with flames and embers, a multitude of madmen shot off fireworks and transformed the night sky into flames and all the stars into embers. Moisés was throwing up foam. And they both closed their eyes as hard as they could, and both saw a perfect blackness swallowing them: not the blackness that comes from lowering the eyelids and that's speckled by luminous dust, nor the blackness of it being night and us imagining, as we go to sleep, the day or even the morning, but the absolute blackness of solitude, indifferent black, absolute solitude, eternal black, eternal solitude. Moisés was throwing up foam that, against his will, rose up in him and issued from his mouth as a round, continuous substance. It wasn't a white foam, for it contained blood and yellowish bits from his insides. And the pain, increasing, became unbearable. And the brothers struggled against the fire that burned more than fire, against the inaudible scream that deafened them, and against the black blackness of death that blinded them, to look at each other one last time. And in that long, significant moment they stopped burning inside, they looked at each other, and they said no words in their gaze; they entered each other, they exchanged bodies, and in that way hugged each other. At the end of that moment Moisés, destroyed, fell dead.

That evening, when they didn't show up for dinner, the cook asked the migrant who lived opposite to go fetch them. It was this man who found Moisés with his head lying on Elias's lap and Elias crying with a face already ravaged by many tears. It was this man who found them in the darkness of the oil press and struck a match to light up their faces, not realizing that it was impossible to light up that darkness. He looked at the water that formed wide rivers on Elias's face, at his eyes that were the springs of those rivers, and saw only that he wept. He didn't see that Elias had experienced death without dying; he didn't see that he had died and survived death to keep suffering. And this man returned with other men in silence, grave and dark men, sad men who lifted Moisés and laid him on a wagon. Elias always at his side, crying. The wagon's iron wheels rolled over the dust and stones of the street, and it was the only sound heard in the night's funereal silence. The wagon rolled and the streets slowly lit up, because every house door opened and everyone, full of sorrow, came out to see the brothers. The men standing in the doorways with their caps off and their arms outstretched, unmoving; next to them their wives, with the same mournful gaze of uncontainable sorrow. The men who had gone to get the brothers walked through the night, themselves like pieces of solemn and black night, pulling the mule by its reins; on top of the wagon lay the corpse of Moisés and bent over it, the ruins of Elias's body, his tears. They walked for many nights in that night to reach the cook's house. And the wagon came to a halt. The widowed cook, dressed in dark black, waited for them at the door, overwhelmed, weeping. Forever in silence, as if they were immobile, the men carried Moisés inside and laid him on the new bedspread. The baby's crib was empty, for as soon as the migrant had returned from the oil press to ask for help, as soon as he had broken the news to the cook and the neighbor women gathered around, one of them took the girl to her house to sleep. The men pulled Moisés's legs together, placed his right arm over his chest, and left. The brothers and the cook were alone, and sadness seized the whole house. Like a shadow above ground, the cook went out and came back with a cloth and a basin. She stripped the brothers, one as spent as the other, and washed them with the cloth that she dipped into the basin. She dried them and clothed them in a pair of fine, very white shirts and in their dress suits. The suits weren't black, but they had no others. She buttoned the gold buttons one by one. She figured out the system of buttons and straps for the joined sleeves and fastened them. She combed the brothers' hair and sat in one of the chairs that the neighbor women had brought and placed around the bed. The light of the kerosene lamp flickered on the room's sorrow until morning. At daybreak the first woman arrived. She expressed her condolences to the widow and to the brother, and no one heard, she propped open the front door with a piece of wood, blew out the lamp, and opened the shutters to the window. Elias wept all that he had ever lived, for his whole life lay dead on a bedspread before him. The cook wept for having lost her husband, realizing, more than ever, how much he meant to her, and that only made her suffer more, for she'd lost forever her friend, the man for whom she lived and whose happiness she so desired. A second woman arrived. After saying my heartfelt condolences, my heartfelt condolences, and staring for a long time at the corpse of Moisés, she sat next to the other woman. One of them whispered it was some poisonous mushrooms that he ate. Elias ran his hand over his brother's eyes and over his brother's lips as very clear tears ran down his own cheeks. The morning entered slowly, sadly, through the window.

$\mathcal{B}$Y THE FINGER THAT JOINS US, your death has entered me like a progressive disease. I feel my hand as cold as yours, I feel your blood passing through the veins of my hand and coldly flowing throughout my body, I feel my body as cold as yours. Brother, I heard you before you died and you can't hear me now. These my words are like words written on a blank sheet that remains blank with those words, invisible since there's no one to read them, words that grow old since there's no one who understands them, words that lose their meaning, blending imperceptibly into a breeze that no one notices. Brother, my gaze is completely wasted, knowing as I do that you see nothing. My gaze is entirely useless in your silence, transforming entirely into that silence that remembers your life and your death. The morning light, silent because you are dead and it was you who gave it a voice; the morning light, illuminating each dark corner as when you smile . . . If now your eyes were open, you would enjoy seeing this morning. It wouldn't be sad, we'd feel this morning on our faces, warming us up. I'd like to be little again and to play with you. To sit with you on the ground and have a morning like this one light up our play and sit down next to us, playing with us and being perhaps our plaything. I'd like to fall asleep with you as when we peacefully fell asleep on nights of an August so distant from this one. We, naked in bed, with the sheet rolled up at our feet and the window open to the night in the backyard, and when the first breeze of early morning entered, we'd wake up at the same time and pull up the sheet, and in those childhood days we slept as long as we wanted, waking up together when the sunlight hit and opened our closed eyes. I'd like to be with you on Senhor Marcos's tract, our father opening furrows with the plow and telling us go and take this bunch of collard greens and this bunch of turnip greens to Senhor Marcos; and when we reached the large door, it was I who lifted the little iron hand holding a ball and struck it against the door, it was you who talked to the housekeeper, saying our father sent us with this bunch of collard greens and this bunch of turnip greens for Senhor Marcos, and the housekeeper would say I'll take them, not thank you, not you needn't have troubled, just I'll take them, and she'd shut the door. Your voice is what I'll never be able to hear again, and I just wish I could hear it say let's rest now, or hear it say brother, brother. Brother. I've cried so much, and last night was the eternity of many suffering lives, the same despair repeated in many despairing lives. I know the taste of tears. Remember when it rained? Remember our father, at the market, buying us two identical black umbrellas? We'd walk down the street with our two umbrellas together, circling around puddles, the rain turning the irrigation ditches into rivers, our two umbrellas together, the rain trickling down from the ribs. My tears remind me of that rain, but your absence from this morning and everything in it makes this morning and everything an encounter with sadness, and there are no tears here that can compare with being in the rain at your side. Everything with you was good because you, brother, were good. And last night killed and buried me. Last night without you was a long time, it was years, many years. I'm older than if I'd died centuries ago, more worn out than if I were now just a memory remembered by no one. You have departed for the eternal place of your infinite solitude and have left me alone in this place of so many people so distant from me. Brother, if as a dead man I could remain attached to you, I'd want to die now so as to keep living. But what I want doesn't count. A night awaits me which is different from and the same as the one you've already entered. For all of us there's a death which, being different from person to person, just as life is different, makes us walk through all that for us is black, through all solitude, screaming out to no one all that we're able to love. Here, the morning, the oblivious mornings. Now and then I look at your body stretched out on the new bedspread that we never used, in this bedroom that isn't ours and where we got used to waking up, and it pains me that you're now cold, it pains me that your skin is limp, it pains me to see people come look at you and you're dead: your gaze never again, your smile never again, you hearing me never again, you existing and being witness to what I was and we were, never again. Brother. The new, still ungreased boots that you were saving for winter but that now cover your feet with the toes pointing

upward, the soles clean and perfect: the boots you wear today
and forever, since they're of no more use here, since nothing that
was yours and that you cared for is of use to anyone anymore.
Your ironed trousers, your jacket, the white shirt with the pointy
tips on the collar. Your transfigured face: its forehead more serene
than any living man's forehead; the eyebrows sparse, since they've
ceased to serve a purpose; the eyelids thick and heavy, covering
forever your blind eyes like a tombstone; the nose lean and inert;
the lips, washed of dried foam and of words and of unconscious
laughs, now thinner, thinner; the useless chin. To look at your
face wearies me inside my weariness. My body and what isn't
my body but still is me, everything in me, I, the black piece of
sky or stone, sky within the interior of a stone, shut up in the
compact solitude of a stone, never having seen the sun, never
having breathed, I, I myself, I am a terminal exhaustion. I'm the
long-distance runner who went around the world to take a letter
to himself and who, now that he found himself, is no longer the
same, and who now, out of breath, desires only to lean over a
precipice and breathe, and they cover his mouth, and many people with many hands cover his mouth. My heart is the emptiness
in the eyes of a condemned man. My shadow is my solitude. I've
wearied all of me out. All my weariness collided with my weariness, and all of me is just this. The night in which you died fell
on what I am. Morning has begun, and last night is a rotting
corpse inside me. Brother, my arms are impotent, and daylight is
the darkness now controlling them. I'm worn out, I'm spent, as if
I'd been trampled by a thousand feet, and I wish I had been trampled by a thousand feet. I'm dead, as if I'd died in the hour you
died, and I wish I had died with you. I'm the one who is only a
brother and has no brother. I'm the one who's still waiting. At
least a final gaze from you, at least the small hope of a final gaze

from you. I've lost everything. We've lost everything, brother. I'm weary. I'm waiting for a word to roll off your lips. Tell me, please, that I can rest.

IT WAS A HUMBLE BEDROOM. With no pictures on the walls, no calendar, no mirror. It was a bedroom of white walls. While the brothers were being brought from the oil press the neighbor women, weaving through the cook's grief, removed the crib from the bedroom, changed the sheets on the bed, and placed as many chairs around it as they could find and that would fit in the room. The women marveled at the size of the bed, and it took three of them to tuck in the sheets and the bedspread. The women moved like ants around the widowed cook, who was lost in the far reaches of her mourning, where she would remain during the watch and the funeral. The widowed cook, Elias, and the deceased Moisés passed the night alone and in silence. When morning broke, their skin looked duller, as if coated by a layer of dust that was a layer of sorrow. And with the day's arrival the first women arrived. Little by little their number swelled, women dressed in black who whispered and looked on with pity. Elias wept until midmorning. Then the tears rolling down his cheeks in meandering paths stopped. His eyes dried, and his face was one of silent, steadfast suffering. When the first men arrived it was already past midmorning, the bedroom was full of women, and Elias was wrapped in silence. In pairs or alone, the men entered with caps in hand, looked at Moisés for a suspended moment, said my heartfelt condolences, my heartfelt condolences, and went out. On the street, near the door, the men stood around in an expanding circle and rolled cigarettes glued with their tongues, pondering their own death while they smoked them, and someone said that's life.

No one from the town had taken the news to the Mount of Olives, but old Gabriel woke up suddenly with a pain in his chest, and the first thing he thought of was Moisés. He solemnly lit the logs in the fireplace with a pinecone. He drank his coffee sitting next to the fire, watching the feminine dance of the flames and waiting for daybreak. The plants were beginning to wake up when old Gabriel set out on the road into town. His mind skirted a path that was full of shadows because full of doubts. We never know all there is to know, he thought. That morning was hiding something from him. He walked through the quiet of the light while repeating to himself: what happened? What on earth happened? His steady gaze saw only the uncertainty that preoccupied him, the certainty that something had happened about which he knew nothing. He walked with quick steps, like scythes cutting swaths of grass. When he'd gone halfway, a cyclone of birds swirled in the sky overhead, but he didn't notice. All the birds flying over the town and the surrounding fields came together in that black-stippled blanket that waved in the sky, held up by thousands of fragile bodies and a rustle of wings. Old Gabriel continued in his blind determination until he saw the town's first house. At that moment the birds all swooped down on him, and despite the resistance of his arms and feet, the sparrows, pigeons, thrushes, swallows, and the other birds wrapped him in a thick cloud and lifted him into the air, into the sky. Flying nearly as high as the clouds, had there been clouds, they soon covered the distance back to the farmstead and set old Gabriel down at his front door. As he watched the birds scatter in the sky and he helplessly extended his arms toward the earth, he realized, with frustration, that there was nothing he could decide. Trapped in his human condition, he fetched his hoe and spent the day in his garden.

By early afternoon there were already many men in front of the door. The heat was excruciating, and the men took cover under a bit of shade. Inside, to keep it cool, one of the shutters on the window had been closed, and the other one half closed. The women, in this half-light, sat in the chairs that lined the wall, while the widowed cook sat in a chair closer to the bed. Elias was standing, with his right arm resting on his dead brother. No one had the courage to propose separating the brothers or even to mention the matter. Whoever saw the two brothers saw two dead men; and the mourning didn't increase, the grief became no greater, when in the late afternoon Elias collapsed on the bed. Dying, for Elias, was the depletion of all his strength. Dying was the unbearable extreme of an absolute exhaustion. An immeasurable silence. An immeasurable nostalgia. After a black moment in everyone's heart, one of the women went outside to call in two men, who stretched Elias out at his brother's side. In death they had the same face, the same color, the same expression. When night had completely darkened the room, someone lit a kerosene lamp, and the women began to leave. Their shadows passed over the brothers' dead bodies, taking a little of that sad room to where they were going. Seven women remained. It wasn't cold, but all of them wore black shawls over their shoulders. It was a very long night. More years than make a life went by on that night. When the tears finally stopped in the eyes of the widowed cook, the approaching morning could already be felt. And it was in an even more painful silence, a silence of her wanting to but not being able to cry, a silence of her feeling only a deep darkness: darkness under darkness under darkness; it was in a black silence that the widowed cook felt the first light of dawn. And once more the women and men arrived. And the widowed cook didn't react to the approaching sound of the wagon that would take the corpses to the cemetery. She didn't react when the men, lugging a huge coffin, entered the bedroom and placed the brothers inside it, side by side. They closed the lid and, with great difficulty, passed through the kitchen to the street and hoisted the coffin with the brothers onto the funeral wagon. Smaller than other wagons, it was painted shiny black and was pulled by two men. Under the unusual weight of the twin-sized coffin, the springs screeched with their lack of flexibility. The widowed cook got up from her chair with the help of two women and, disconsolate and lifeless, made the long walk to the cemetery. And every street, everything she saw, reminded her of the brothers, of the happiest year of her life, of the little house she'd loved, of the life she'd wanted to build, of the hours she'd spent cooking for the brothers and imagining their smiles when they arrived, everything reminded her of the plans she'd made for the little girl, whom they would never see as a grown woman. The widowed cook was very old and had nothing. When they reached the cemetery, the sun was a dull reflection of itself in the sky. Next to the grave, the coffin was reopened. The brothers' faces, their best suits. Then, dirt. Shovelfuls of dirt that made, first, the sound of metal blades stabbing a mound of dirt and then, once hurled into the air, the unmistakable sound of dirt when it hits the wood of a coffin, with much of the memory of those corpses that were once people being buried forever. Surrounded by women who helped her but all alone, the widowed cook returned to the town. They took her to the house of the neighbor who was watching the little girl. The widowed cook looked at the baby, who couldn't understand, and tried with very sincere eyes to tell her everything. And she hugged the baby with all her might before losing her mind.

J OSÉ'S SHEEPDOG WAS LYING
down, neck raised, in a noble pose and with a serene expression,
ears stretched out, eyes closed, as if she were feeling the softness
of the breeze. And she was feeling the softness of the breeze: a
delicate wall, a very thin veil that passed by imperceptibly, the
memory of a sheet of glass slowly crossing the plain. In the
shade, half dozing, the sheep chewed on the dry grass in the par-
ticular way sheep chew: by moving their jaws horizontally, in opposite directions. José stood still on his feet, chest leaning against
his staff, musing. He'd slept badly the night before, tortured by
strange ideas. Lying in bed, his eyes open to the darkness, he listened to his wife's breathing and to the quicker breathing of their

son, and he thought of his wife and of the giant, he thought of his wife embracing the giant and of the giant abusing her, over and over, over and over. He suddenly envisioned his wife with the giant, thinking: it can't be true. He took momentary comfort in this thought, but soon his wife's face and the giant's face rematerialized in his mind, the pure body of his wife mixed up with the repugnant body of the giant. Once, just once, he reached the point of thinking: and if the baby isn't my son? But he felt a very deep pit in his chest, a seemingly bottomless pit of fear, and immediately he thought: it can't be true. A profound horror prevented him from returning to that idea, but within him lurked the shadow: the black, almost hazy outline of that thought: the constant, inexorable presence of a dagger he wanted to pull out of his heart. Certainty is made of many doubts, a certainty is made of a thousand times a thousand doubts, and nothing is worse than a doubt, thought José. Next to the sheep, with his chest leaning against the staff, he mused about such things as this. And the afternoon lent itself to musing. The hottest part of the day was dissolving more slowly than the eyes of men could see. The plains were becoming more endless.

With a whistle that cut through the air like a whip, José called the dog. The tips of her ears lifted as if pulled by a fishing line, her eyes opened as if she'd smelled game, and she leapt from her spot as if to run after a hare. And she barked at the legs of the sheep. The sheep, startled, woke up to a nightmare which, in their not very intelligent sheep minds, they quickly forgot, falling into line and moving forward as a herd, always forward, since the legs of sheep can't move backward. And the proud, haughty, almost human sheepdog proceeded to the farmstead at José's side. It was earlier than usual when the sheep, goaded by barks that pierced the air, entered through the gate. It was summer, it was August, and the longer day still had a lot of afternoon to go. The air was sheer light. José crossed the courtyard, but only entered the house in his mind: he looked at his wife, who didn't look back, and he wanted to tell her something that he didn't say and that she didn't hear. With the black sheepskin on his back and the sack slung over his shoulder by a rope, he passed by the closed door of old Gabriel and proceeded toward the town. He pictured old Gabriel and pictured Moisés, and both images splintered into a swarm of colors, an explosion of colors in the face and body of Moisés; both standing before him and saying things he couldn't make out with his blind ears, his deaf eyes. And he wished he could have heard Moisés and old Gabriel now, and he wished that the world weren't an irreversible fall, in which you just keep on falling, forever closer to the depths, forever farther from the light. He proceeded toward the town. Not because he wanted to reach it. Not because he wanted, but because of the afternoon, because of the sun and light, because of an overwhelming solitude.

The sheepdog followed him, with a gaze that looked up from her bowed head. A vast gaze, like a soft, brown sky. A child's or a mother's gaze that was nevertheless a dog's gaze. They reached the town. José thought. My wife. The giant. José thought my wife, the giant, and the people who saw him pass by didn't say good afternoon, because they all recognized his grief and condemnation, his suffering. He reached the square, and his shadow, sweeping the ground, was firm, for it was a shadow that knew where it was going. Dogs from many different directions came and surrounded the sheepdog, wooing her in a now courteous, now bestial fashion. José walked straight toward Judas's general store and entered alone. The devil, at the counter, looked at him from inside a smile. José looked at him without smiling and advanced. Looking at each other squarely, intently, without veering their eyes, holding on to the iron bar of their gazing, the devil said two glasses of red. Two full glasses appeared on the marble counter. Drink up. And José, engrossed in the devil's fiery eyes, didn't budge. The devil, looking at him across the top of his glass, smiled as he drank and, after a studied pause, said your wife isn't who you think she is. José, inwardly consumed by a shudder, remained impassive. And the tempter, smiling, said if you don't believe me, go home and see for yourself, the shutters of the bedroom window are open, just take a look through the crack in the curtains. José walked past the tables and out the door, the men dropped their arms and gazes, the devil smiled broadly, and the brimming glass of red wine remained on the counter by itself, like a witness of that moment, like an orphan, like a lit candle. José crossed the square, and the sheepdog looked at him and whimpered, but despite her desperate attempts she couldn't follow him, for she was surrounded by a number of suddenly disinterested dogs, and joined to a dog whose tongue hung out.

On the road to the Mount of Olives José's boots stepped more quickly. They made the rough sound of shovels digging into a pile of sand, moving fast and hard enough to hurl grains of sand far behind them. Seen from the sky, José was a speck advancing along a furrow cut into the plain, or a dot with arms and legs advancing along a furrow that cut between two plains or between two diversely colored parts of the same plain. Seen from the sky, José was next to nothing, and he didn't even think it can't be true, it can't be true, nor did he hurry. Seen from the sky, all that he thought and that for him loomed larger than the sky was less than the feather of a swallow among the clouds or the memory of a raindrop on a stormy day. He had almost reached the

to where men cease being men. I'm going to take the lonely road that wends through life's wreckage. The road where everything is scarcely anything, and each tiny thing is too much. At my side lie the vestiges of days with sheep and thoughts I don't remember. At my side lie bits of you, of my son, of my father, my mother, my sister. You hanging up laundry, you on the devil's lips, on everybody's lips, abortion, she had an abortion, sweet girl, lying under the giant, feeding our son, sweet girl, sweet girl, your soft skin, that late afternoon we made love. My son when just born, with his serious, infant gaze, the first time I held him in my arms, in my heart, such a warm thing, sleeping in his crib. My father faithfully teaching me all he knew, hitting me with his belt, crying, pulling up on his trousers, looking at me and talking to me, sitting in front of my sister's chicken coop, taking me with him into Judas's general store, taking me to the cattle fair. My mother sending me into town on errands, giving me kisses, dying in bed, alive, then dead, in the coffin, telling me stories in the backyard. My sister helping my mother, wanting to get married, playing grown-ups and children all by herself, my mother prancing around her while sticking pins into her dress, the hopeful glimmer in her eyes, always talking, taking care of our father, getting married to the blacksmith who was drunk at the wedding, weeping, taking care of their child with awkward tenderness. I walk alone but have all of you with me. I'll take you with me always. I look at the last ray of sun before the sun disappears. I think: a man is a day, a man is the sun for one day. And he has to keep going. My feet move forward over the earth. You're still sleeping, my son, and I wanted to show you the sunset. I wanted to show you the earth, to teach you the color of earth on the inside, because to know the color of earth on the inside is to know the world and to know men. Now the sun has disappeared, leaving a bloodred aura over the summit where it sank, and I wanted to teach you that tomorrow will be a hot day. I wanted to teach you, son, that if you don't see stars at night, you can expect rain the next day. To know these things is to know everything. These are the few things we're given to know. The rest, son, are inscrutable mysteries. The rest are pointed daggers in the fog. The rest are daggers we see flying toward our chest, and our hands are tied, son. You're still sleeping. Your mother has me in her gaze. I have her gaze. Wife, who watches and sees me, know that I respect you. And in telling you this I'm telling you many things I don't understand, I'm telling you of a red sky over the summit of my heart, I'm telling you what I feel even if it's impossible to tell what we feel. And what you are in me will be crystallized in the face I become. And you won't be a bitter regret, you'll be the sweet girl I saw hanging up laundry. You'll be what I wrote in the notebooks of my yearning to have you, the notebooks I know by heart, for they're the pages of my own skin. Saturday, six p.m., she watered the garden, held a rose in her fingers, smiled to herself. Friday, five thirty p.m., she came out of the rich people's house, looking at the ground. Thursday, five p.m., she came to the door, the skin of her face so peaceful, her eyes like the sky. And wherever I end up, I won't be able to touch you, as I've never been able. And my frustration will be greater, since I'll never again be able to see you, never again be able to hear your silence, and all the hopes I ever had will be obliterated. When dead, I'll know the absolute blackness that no living man can bear. Not one gleam. Not one glimmer. No man alive can bear darkness without a glimmer of light. And that's why I must keep walking. Just a few more yards separate me from the endless infinite distance of that place. My suffering will be a continuation of suffering. I'll continue not to have the will that I never had. And my steps are no longer mine, nor were they ever. Everything is final. The fields have lasted one more day, and tomorrow doesn't exist. The red sky will remain forever red, and the sky I once knew will forever be a memory of what I once knew. Goodbye, wife. Goodbye, son. Goodbye, father, mother, sister. Your faces hover before me. They will hover there forever. I think: forever and never again are the same place. Wife, son, father, mother, sister, don't cry for me. The wheat fields still exist for children. Children still exist. Save your tears for a worthier occasion. Save your tears for when the wheat fields die in the eyes of children. Save your tears for when the children die. Today, I'm dying. And my death is nothing in the implacable order of things.

JOSÉ APPROACHED THE GNARLED HOLM OAK, the only one on the hilltop. It was a holm oak whose trunk zigzagged this way and that. José patiently made a slipknot in the rope, then tied the rope firmly around a strong bough. He climbed to one of the steps in the trunk. He placed the noose around his neck and tightened it. He didn't look at the world for one last time. He jumped forward. His neck made a cracking sound of bones separating. He swung for a few moments until coming to a standstill, as still as the unstirring breeze. A sparrow that flitted about looked at him and saw his eyes emptied of hope, saw his hands empty, and swooped up into the sky. José became smaller, smaller, and when the sparrow looked down from on high, José was just the gnarled bough of an oak tree against a bloodred horizon.

book two

HE EARTH WAS ITS OWN SI-
lence on fire. The sun was a blazing heat lighting up the flame-
colored air: the aura of a fire that was the aura of the earth, that
was the light and the sun. The small stones and weightless pebbles dotting the skin of the plain were hot embers in a closed fist.
José and his sheep, the sheepdog, the big old cork tree, and the
smaller corks were figures etched into an exhausted asphyxia,
shapes frozen in the blaze of an instant that was a very long time
and no more than an instant. The south wind blew through a
wheat field, and its blowing shriveled the stalks of grain, suddenly old and dry, because that slow breeze was a sweltering hell
that filled the atmosphere, forcing all breathing things to breathe

it, since there was nothing around them but that heavy, scorching breeze. And the south wind was the horizon advancing, slow and inevitable. Inevitable. It blew past the last stalk at the end of the field, drying it out even more, then past a clump of thistles that withered beneath and inside its heat. José could be seen in the distance, standing in the shade of the big old cork tree, and the sheep could be seen, gathered into little bunches of many little bodies in the shade. The south wind advanced within the light and over the earth. José and the sheep were slowly drawing closer together. Closer and closer. And the south wind blew past José and past the sheep and past the big old cork tree and the smaller corks. In the south wind every gaze persisted, skin scorched, blood seething.

I KNOW THIS STILLNESS. I know this afternoon. The sheep lying, as if dead, under the cork trees. The sheepdog lying at my feet. The thin grass bending at the slightest breeze. The sky meeting the earth, which mirrors the sky's languor, which mirrors the earth's languor. I know this afternoon, for I've lived it many times, for I've listened many times to this stillness and this calm certainty. I think: perhaps there's a light inside men, perhaps a clarity, perhaps men are not made of darkness, perhaps certainties are a breeze inside men, and perhaps men are the certainties they possess.

A burning where my heart is tells me that he's coming. He's walking this way. I feel in my body his body walking, his footsteps neither fast nor slow. I feel in my body his simple ideas and sincere intentions. I feel in my face his manly and boyish expression, the expression of a boy who had to hurry into manhood. He's coming. And when the afternoon relents and the heat becomes milder, he'll arrive. Coming from the direction of the

farmstead, he'll arrive and, seeing me, he'll start running, the
way a fearful child runs to his mother's arms. And as if we were
embracing, he'll look at me with his forever sincere eyes. He'll
believe in me. And he'll go away with the peacefulness of simple
souls. While I, as the dying afternoon slips into an almost nocturnal transparency, will be the torment I'm used to, the chaos of
my sorrows and hopes. And here, under this sky touching me
with its fire, I already know that's how it will be. A burning
where my heart is tells me so.

JOSÉ WAS THE SON OF JOSÉ. He had his father's name and knew
the few things he'd been told about him in answer to the few
questions he'd asked. He knew he was just like him, forever since
he was a little boy old Gabriel had told him you look and act just
like your father. No one ever had the courage to tell José how
his father had died, and he'd learned from his mother's doleful
mourning that it was something he shouldn't talk about. José
hadn't heard much about his father, but he'd figured out everything. On afternoons like that one, in which he waited for Salomão while tending the sheep, José had realized he was the son
of a great and sad love. He'd discerned his father's face when he
saw his own face reflected in the pool on the farmstead. You look
and act just like your father, old Gabriel said when he played in
the dirt in the yard, when he arrived from the fields in the afternoon, when he visited the blind prostitute for the first time. And
José knew it was true, for he'd discerned a force within his force,
identical gestures within each of his gestures.

And José, the son of José, waited for Salomão. The big old
cork tree tried to wrap him up with its tiny leaves, as it had tried
to wrap his father thirty years earlier; the earth all around him
burned, as it had burned around his father thirty years earlier;

the hazy, sad sheep looked at him from out of the corner of their eyes, as they'd looked at his father thirty years earlier, but José didn't know or even think about this. Holding the staff with his left hand, he repeated to himself what he knew: he's coming. The sheepdog, the big old cork tree, and the sheep were so utterly familiar with that afternoon that they remembered it even before it happened. They knew at precisely what moment Salomão would appear on the horizon. Stretched out as if sleeping, the very old sheepdog remembered the night when, thirty years earlier, she'd seen her owner hanging from the gnarled holm oak on Gallows Tree Hill; and she remembered going back to the town and rounding up all the dogs on the square; she remembered how they waited patiently, how they waited, waited, and how, when the massive figure of the giant emerged from Judas's general store, they followed him down the dark streets, scarcely lit by a starry night. Under the darkness of her eyelids she remembered that night from thirty years ago, she remembered how her body and the bodies of all the other dogs pounced on the giant and knocked him down, she remembered the deafening sound of all the dogs growling, she remembered the sensation of her teeth ripping into an ear, her teeth ripping out an eye, her teeth opening a hole in his chest, tearing open a corner of his mouth. She remembered the giant's body in pieces on the ground, the warm taste of his blood; she remembered the solitary road to the Mount of Olives, and the night; she remembered lying down and waiting at the door of José's house; she remembered hearing the little boy cry now and then. The very old sheepdog waited for Salomão, as she had waited for the giant thirty years earlier.

The sheepdog raised her head, which had been resting against her front paws. The heat in the air slowly mingled with the earth's coolness. The sun no longer yellowed the sky. The light was now ethereal. A worldwide silence loomed on the horizon. The moment had arrived. José shifted his sharp gaze, fixing it in the direction of the farmstead.

MY FOOTSTEPS DREW NEAR JUDAS'S GENERAL STORE, and the hubbub of the men playing cards and drinking and talking formed a ball of voices that slowly rolled across the square, as if pushed by the slow breeze. I went in and said good evening before reaching the counter. Yes, I said good evening. The men from this corner and that corner, all with the same face, answered good evening, Salomão. I distinctly remember that sputter of good evenings, for it was the first time I'd noticed it. It sometimes happens that I suddenly notice something that was always there, and the time of my noticing becomes for me the first time, which I always remember later, should I think about that thing. And so it was with that disparate outburst of voices, some soft and others loud, some lively and others bored, some quick and some sluggish. I went up to the counter. A glass of red wine. Next to me four men stood around an enamel plate with a thin strip of fried bacon; they were drinking wine, and each time one of them wielded the dull blade of the jackknife to cut a paper-thin sliver of bacon, he did it with great ceremony as the others looked on, feasting their eyes. Judas's son, sleeves rolled up, went from group to group, clearing away empty glasses and participating in all the conversations. I caught his attention. A glass of red wine. I set my empty glass on the counter. And in that isolated moment there was a fearful silence. The men who were talking hushed. The men picking at food stepped back. Behind me stood the devil. I felt his warmth and smile against my back. Two glasses of red wine, he said, smiling. The glasses, full to the brim, appeared before us. He raised his glass and drank it down, looking and smiling at me with his eyes. My glass stood there untouched, gleaming. The men looked at me. The devil looked at me, looked at me, smiling, and said I haven't seen your wife around, where is she? I moved three steps down the counter. He moved with me. The silence was the suffocation one must feel before dying. Before dying from choking, and you want to breathe, to grab air with your arms, to stuff globs of air into your mouth, to stick your fingers down your throat, and it's blocked, you're choking to death. You know, said the tempter while smiling, your cousin José told me he knows better than you where she is, at this very moment and always. I took two steps backward. The men looked at me with speechless astonishment. The devil looked at me and smiled, he smiled. With a broad grin, as big as the whole store, he said your cousin José told me he has more control over her than you do. Is that true, Salomão? A dim cloud of luminous smoke cast a pall on the light, and a whirlwind of mirrors rose up and showed me to everyone everywhere, when all I wanted to do was hide. Is it true, Salomão? The men looked at me. The devil looked at me. My legs were a pile of loose sand, holding up a brick house being thrashed by high winds. Is it true, Salomão? I ran out fleeing across the square. The devil's smile at the door of the general store. The night darker than before. The streets empty. I entered my house, entered the bedroom, took off my clothes, and lay down next to my wife, trembling.

SALOMÃO WALKED ON THE PATH that went from the farmstead to the pasture where José tended the sheep. Behind him lay the road from the town to the farmstead, weariness, the sun. With him went the memory of what he'd heard the night before, fear, weariness, the sun. Salomão walked, and in his face another face frowned, in his fear another fear lurked, in himself there was another. He carried a burden. He walked and the silence became an ever-heavier, ever-closer silence, a silence that kept repeating words, repeating to him the same words over and over. Last night. The words from last night. Words. Night, last night. Words. Words. Words. Everything blended into a whirl of confusion in his head. Everything combined and confronted him in a storm of transfiguring mirrors. Salomão walked and did not understand. He hurried. He stopped. He hurried. And the voices all whirling in his head. Last night. Words words words.

Salomão was the son of José's father's sister. Salomão was older than his cousin José, but he never acted like it. They played together as children, and it was always José who led their games, who decided what they should do and where they should go. José liked to climb trees, but Salomão was afraid; José liked to play hide-and-seek, but it frightened Salomão to be alone; José liked to play tag, but Salomão could never catch him. When Salomão talked about José, he called him cousin; when José talked about Salomão, he called him Salomão.

Once past the farmstead, when he saw the last summit and knew that José and the sheep were on the other side, he hastened his step, running awkwardly, like someone with a limp, like a limping child.

I THINK: PERHAPS THE SKY is a huge sea of fresh water and we, instead of walking under it, walk on top of it; perhaps we see everything upside down and the earth is a kind of sky, so that when we die, when we die, we fall and sink into the sky.

THE TWILIGHT PAUSED. The last remnants of afternoon, a peaceful canticle, stood still. The last light of day glowed hard and fast.

The birds' singing lapsed into a cruel melody of silence. The breeze halted, still cool. Salomão slowly came into view on the summit, as if climbing a set of stairs: his head, his chest, waist, legs. José watched him. When at last the whole of him appeared, Salomão began running with clumsy steps, not stumbling but as if he were stumbling, as if he were very fat. Nearing José, he slowed down and they clearly saw each other's face. Salomão said is it true, José? A moment went by, and José did not look at him. Salomão relaxed his face, as if it had been greatly straining, and told what had happened the night before. The words. José listened. Finally, with night still on the far side of that splendorous glowing, Salomão said it's not true, is it? I know it's not. Salomão looked at him with a look that was a manly embrace. And he left. He vanished behind the summit in the direction of the homestead. José looked at the sky. The birds' singing resumed its mysterious symmetry. The breeze resumed its dry, torrid substance. The afternoon lingered enough to be crossed by a swallow. And the night fell.

HE MORNING ENTERED
through the open windows, filling up the whole kitchen. Salomão's wife bustled about the dining table, rushed out to the
yard to check on her mother, went to the stove to stir the soup,
then back to the table. Salomão woke up late. He left without
drinking any coffee, since there was no coffee to drink. He said
see you later, and his wife, awake since the first sounds of morning, had already bathed her mother, scrubbed the floor, washed
a tub of laundry, and started the soup. Without thinking of José,
Salomão ran through the streets as if his boots were very heavy
or very large. When he entered Master Rafael's carpentry shop,
he automatically took off his cap and waited. Master Rafael

looked at him indifferently, grabbed the pencil from behind his ear, and drew two lines on a board. The first words he said were bring me the chisel and give me a hand here. Salomão put his cap back on and made haste.

The shop wasn't very big for two carpenters and an apprentice. There was a small lumberyard, full of piled-up boards and with pine chips carpeting the ground. Mornings in the yard were a beautiful sight. The sunlight flowed like liquid, softly, without ever scorching; it passed through the grass that sprouted from under the pine chips, and this was soothing. Afternoons were arduous. The same sun was different, beating down on the men's naked backs as they sawed. The sweat seethed on their skin. In the shop itself there were two carpenter's benches and a table in the middle. Master Rafael's bench was neat and clean; his tools were in his toolbox, each one in its place and everything in order. Salomão's bench was cluttered and covered with shavings and sawdust; his tools were wherever he'd left them last, everything a mess. The table in the middle, full of slits for the saws, unintentional holes made by drills or by nails, and dents from straying hammers, was used by both of them to work on larger pieces. In one corner, next to the earthen jug with streaks of lime running down the neck, there were two shelves crammed with boxes of nails, and although nothing was written on them, Master Rafael would say give me two eightpenny nails, or give me three finishing nails, or give me three tenpenny ribbed nails, and Salomão knew exactly which ones they were, he'd hand them over, and this was all natural. But that morning there was no whistling, no conversation. They worked in silence.

It was close to lunch hour when Master Rafael said to the apprentice you can go to lunch. Taking one step with his crutch and another with his leg, he turned to Salomão. It was from his father that Master Rafael had inherited the carpenter's shop, along with his stiff manners and sincerity of feelings. His father had taught him all he knew, about wood and about everything else. He lived in the small house that had been his father's. And all the jobs he completed, with Saturdays and Sundays likewise spent in the shop, earned him only enough for his sustenance and a fortnightly visit to the house of the blind prostitute. There were several other carpenters in the town, but no one knew as much about his trade as Master Rafael. His father had taught him everything. He was born the day his mother died and, although he did not know it, his father had looked at him with watery eyes and said I'm going to make you into a man. Master Rafael's right leg ended right below the groin, his right arm was just a stump into which the top of his crutch fit snugly, he was missing his right ear and was blind in his right eye. He was a man. At ten years of age, he helped his father in the carpenter's shop like a grown-up. His father beamed with pride. He smiled. His father died on the day he saw his son turn into a man. And now, on that morning, he hobbled through the wood shavings toward Salomão and said what's the matter? Salomão didn't answer right away but looked at him affectionately and finally said it's all taken care of.

THE MORNING ENTERS THROUGH THE OPEN WINDOWS, filling up the whole kitchen. The soup is done, I take it off the stove, and now I feel like resting. Salomão will enter by that door over there. Maybe he'll look at me. He won't say a word, for we've never talked, and now it's too late. He'll crumble crusts of bread into his bowl, cover them with soup, and eat in silence, looking at the table. That's when I'll go out to the yard. I'll pull my mother into a corner, tuck a bib into her collar, and feed her spoonfuls of soup as she blankly gazes with her doll-like eyes. With the edge of the spoon I'll catch the broth that drips down her chin, mixed with saliva, and stick it back into her mouth with the next spoonful. My mother will swallow the soup without tasting it, since she'll never stop mumbling the words she's been repeating for thirty years. And the words will make bubbles of soup at the corners of her mouth, and sometimes she'll choke.

From the back door I look at her, surrounded by her toys: her little pots and little pans and little dishes. I remember when I bought them for her. After I got married, I scrimped here and there for six months, until I had enough to buy her the little set of kitchenware. Accustomed to working with sticks and wires, she grabbed the pieces one by one, and spent all afternoon admiring them. Salomão didn't notice the change, and I said nothing to him. I look at her. The shade has moved and she's sitting in the sun. Wherever I put her is where she stays. She fills the little pots with dirt, pebbles, and grass, and sculpts fantastic shapes. I've seen her make the rich people's house at the Mount of Olives, I've seen her make the outside and inside of the church, I've seen her make the entire cemetery. But more than anything else, for many years now, I've seen her make over and over the face of a man, over and over the face of a man or many men with the same face. And she repeats her story. For thirty years now she has repeated her story, the same story. Always. An interminable refrain that begins where it ends, that begins in each word, which never ends. Like an ongoing prayer made of monotonic words, like a humming or a buzzing, like a flying insect, like an eternal housefly, like the inside of a gnat. All day long. All night long. Before falling asleep I always hear her, forming the same words, the same refrain, the same story: not with her voice but with her breathing. For thirty years now. Mother, mother. Her face far away, here. The shade has moved, you're sitting in the sun.

WHEN SALOMÃO LEFT THE CARPENTER'S SHOP, he felt its intense smell of wood slowly give way to the smells from the street and to the sun. Women appeared in the doorways to empty buckets of water and wished him a good day. Salomão thought of José and remembered going to see him at the Mount of Olives, and how they spent hours and hours running in the field and playing. The first time he saw his cousin was at their grandfather's funeral. Salomão was six years old. Without letting go of his arm, his mother introduced him to José. She tried to make them kiss each other, but José turned his head away. Salomão's most vivid memory of their grandfather's funeral, from start to finish, was the face of that little boy looking at him with pride and alarm, that little boy who was his cousin. And he remembered well enough the rest of the funeral: the women who didn't cry much, who patted him on the head and face and neck, saying is this his grandson?, is this his grandson?; his mother who, dressed in black, would cry now and then, to be drowned out immediately by a group of women; and the forbidden sensation that his mother was crying not for her father's death but for her own sorrows, just her own sorrows. And he remembered the old men at the front door, looking solemn and with caps in hand, and he remembered the women saying it was no kind of life, whispering it's terrible to outlive your own son. He remembered thinking about his grandfather in the rare moments when he succeeded in being left alone in his chair. Next to that body now lying there dead, he thought of his grandfather's perfectly still face. Next to that body now lying there dead, he thought of his grandfather's perfectly still face, his perfectly still gaze in front of the chicken coop. And Salomão understood the silence inhabiting that entire body, he learned to understand it on all the mornings when he was six years old. And Salomão thought of the light glancing off the skin of his grandfather on the days when he played with him, all around him, as if he were a doll or a tree. And he thought of the day before the funeral, when he came inside from his games in the backyard and said, unfrightened and lighthearted, unaware of the effect his words would have, grandpa stopped breathing. At six years of age, Salomão didn't grasp the difference between his grandfather breathing or not breathing. Sitting next to his body during the watch through the night, Salomão thought his mother had laid him down in bed, as she did every night, and he didn't understand why people came to see him and said poor man, and whispered it was for the best. He remembered everything, but he remembered with perfect, absolute, crystalline clarity the grown-up gaze of that boy who was his cousin. This is your cousin, said his mother, and behind them the men were throwing spadefuls of dirt over their grandfather. People shoved one another in the wide passageway leading to the exit, to the tall and black and heavy gate, the gate that reached up to the sky. She said this is your cousin, and she purposely didn't say good day to José's mother or even look at her. José's mother was a black place, covered with black. She was the place of no gesture with her hands, no expression on her lips, no gaze in her eyes. José's mother was a very thick, very cold, and very deep fog. She was a dead woman's breathing, a dead woman's skin, faceless, expressionless, with night in her eyes. And on that morning, with the mothers mutually ignoring each other and the boys having nothing to say to each other, the four of them walked together to

José's gravestone. His wife stood there bent over, abstract; his son lowered his eyes and pressed his hands together in front of his stomach; his sister took a handkerchief from her pocket and passed it over the letters of his name; and Salomão looked at them all. And when his mother pulled him away by the arm, when they had returned to the gate of the cemetery, José and his mother were still standing next to the gravestone. Salomão abruptly emerged from the depths of these memories. He suddenly felt all the sun and heat like a comfort. He was already almost home. He remembered José one last time. And he went on, tired, satisfied, a child.

Salomão's wife had pulled her mother back into the shade. And while the widowed cook rearranged her delirious concoctions prepared from earth and pebbles and grass and twigs, her daughter stood there and looked at her. She was very old. The skin of her face was crumpled into a thick mass of wrinkles; she had no teeth, but from endlessly repeating the same conversations her tongue had been cut up by her gums; her hands were skin and bones; and her breasts, as her daughter knew from giving her baths, were two sacks of skin, long and empty. She was very old. When the sun began to set, old Gabriel said that the cook must be more than a hundred years old. In his opinion, she was the oldest person in the town after himself. Old Gabriel was the only one who visited her. And despite being at least one hundred thirty or one hundred fifty years old, Gabriel would arrive a little before day's end. He would arrive looking rested and with a still-fresh bunch of collard greens or spinach under his arm, as if he didn't even feel the long walk from the farmstead to the town. Salomão's wife would take a stool from the stove and place it in the yard for him, and he would sit there listening and looking at the widowed cook. He said nothing to her, because he knew she was shut up inside a bygone time, and because he didn't have anything to say to her. At sundown Salomão's wife would come into the yard balancing a glass of water with both hands. Old Gabriel would drink it voraciously, in a long moment when nothing else existed. Handing her back the glass, he would say something. Usually he would say your mother must be more than a hundred years old, she's the oldest person in town after me. Salomão's wife would go back into the house and he'd follow. They'd cross through the kitchen and she'd open the door to the street. Before leaving, old Gabriel would say see you tomorrow and then walk by himself down the deserted street. He would say see you tomorrow, because they saw each other every day. Every other day she went to the farmstead to clean the rich people's house; on the other days he came to town to visit the widowed cook. Lifting her gaze and letting it fall to the ground like a dead leaf, Salomão's wife remembered that on that afternoon she would also trudge to the farmstead. She entered the kitchen and set out the bowl, the spoon, and the bread. She waited for the moment she knew all too well. Unstartled, she heard Salomão jiggle the door latch.

I DON'T REMEMBER FOR CER-
tain what other thoughts I had, but what I do know is that, just
as soon as I woke up, before getting out of bed and with the
sheets still warm, the first thing I thought about was her face.
Her gaze has both the tormented weariness of Elias and the
blithe energy of Moisés, the silence of Elias and the voice of
Moisés. I noticed this yesterday, when she came outside bringing
a glass of water and a look that smiled and was sad. When I got
her a job at the rich people's house, she looked at me in the same
way. That was the day the sons of Doctor Mateus made a surprise visit and I didn't recognize his children in those men with
neckties, talking so confidently and looking at me warily. I asked

them about Doctor Mateus, and he'd died. I asked them about
his wife, and she'd died. They said they'd come to get acquainted
with the farmstead. This astonished me, since they were born
here, but I said nothing, because I know how short people's
memories are. They wanted to see the little garden, because the
doctor's wife had apparently spent the last years of her senility
talking about it. They wanted to see the flock of sheep. They also
saw, without interest, the vegetable patch. And before they left to
see the fields and farmlands, they wanted to enter the house they
said was theirs. José's mother was locked up inside it. I knocked
on the front door. I banged with my fists. I banged with the
palms of my hands. The sons of Doctor Mateus looked at me. I
said I think she's coming. And I went around the house, banging
on all the windows and all the doors. And I went around the
house again. We waited. We heard some very faint steps approaching. And she opened the door. She had the gaze of a
corpse. Her skin was pale white and stood out from the deep
black of her mourning. She had an intensely dark gaze. Her hair
was gray and unkempt. We went in, and all the windows were
closed. We breathed a foul air, an air that had been there a long
time, that reminded me of Doctor Mateus and his wife. There
was dust on the cabinets and tables and all the furniture, and the
dust was like a second skin on the objects. Cobwebs, thick like
lace tablecloths, hung from the corners of the walls and criss-
crossed the hallways. The floorboards wheezed or groaned as we
walked. Doctor Mateus's sons looked at each other in terror but
said nothing. And as we walked deeper into the house, the stench
grew. It was like the smell of a decaying animal, and we were
walking toward it. The cracks in the walls seemed to spread before our eyes, and when we entered the main hallway, we realized where all the stench was coming from. In front of the voice

shut up inside a trunk there was a stool, and all around, up and down the hallway, were piles of excrement, some dry and some fresh, and the smell of urine and feces was powerful and nauseating. Doctor Mateus's sons, except for the youngest one, had handkerchiefs to cover their mouths. And it was the youngest one who wasn't able to keep from retching, and he vomited a mushy stream on the floor of the main hallway. They ran out of the house, and when I caught up with them outside, still getting their wind back, one of them said we want you to find someone else to take care of the house. We want the house to be like when our parents were alive. That same day I spoke with her. She wasn't yet married to Salomão and began working the next day. She comes here every other day. This afternoon, right after lunch, she'll show up at the gate to the farmstead, mumble a faint good afternoon to me, and continue on her way. Today, when I woke up, I thought about her face.

I CAME HERE FOR THE FIRST TIME just one week after turning seventeen. Already on that day I took note of the olive tree I'm noticing now. It isn't a special olive tree or different from any other, but on that day everything was special and different. I noticed that olive tree. Today I notice it because I remember that day. Old Gabriel had told me the previous evening that there was work for me to do at the farmstead, and that night I rested easy. He told me not to go there until the afternoon, and the sun on that day, like today, was fire on my skin. For my birthday Tiago's wife had given me three skirts she could no longer wear and a scarf she didn't like. I took the scarf out of the suitcase, ironed it, and wrapped it around my head. It smelled new and was soft: it was the first time I wore it. And to this day I wear it: faded, worn, and rough. The distance seemed shorter to me than it does today, and when I reached the Mount of Olives, old Gabriel dropped what he was doing and joined me. We headed to the rich people's house, and the closer we got the larger it loomed in my eyes. Old Gabriel showed me which keys to use, and while he struggled with a huge key to open the severely rusted lock, José's mother peered at us from the concealing depths of her own face. With a gaze at once desperate, threatening, and afraid. We entered. It took a while for our recently sunlit eyes to get used to the absolute darkness, but when I began to see, I realized it was an abandoned but very wealthy house. Old Gabriel told me to cover my mouth and nose. I took the scarf from my head and we entered the main hallway. Without speaking, old Gabriel stopped to look, as if looking were showing, as if showing were explaining. And the voice shut up inside a trunk suddenly said: the wind passes and remains in the leaves that still tremble after it's gone; no man can stop the wind, because all men are part of the wind. We retreated from the main hallway, and old Gabriel said don't be afraid, it's just a voice. I spent that afternoon hauling away buckets of feces. I'd scoop it up with a shovel, cross through the house with a bucket in each hand, and empty them into the wheelbarrow. When the wheelbarrow was full, I'd wheel it to the vegetable patch and dump it onto a compost pile that old Gabriel would use for fertilizer. Tying the scarf around my face to cover my mouth and nose, I stopped a few times to listen to the voice shut up inside a trunk and I began to understand why José's mother had wanted to spend so much time there. Once when I listened I heard it say: perhaps there's a light inside men, perhaps a clarity, perhaps men are not made of darkness, perhaps certainties are a breeze inside men, and perhaps men are the certainties they possess.

That afternoon I met José. He had just finished shutting the sheep inside the sheepfold and walked in my direction. His gaze was steady, almost fierce; meek, like a child's; embarrassed, for being the gaze of a shepherd busy with sheep all day and far away from people; clear. And when he said good afternoon, he already knew who I was. I hesitated just slightly before answering good afternoon, and I also knew who he was. For a week I did nothing at the farmstead but haul filth out of the main hallway. I spent a lot of time sitting next to the voice shut up inside a trunk, listening. And at day's end, when I was getting ready to go back home, José would arrive and say good afternoon. And those simple words said so much, and more each day. Good afternoon, like a sliver of that waning brilliance, like all the silence of sundown and of the earth beneath that ephemeral and yet eternal light. Good afternoon, and his face full of words, and I breathing them in like a breeze. Good afternoon, and the sky. And on my way home the whole expanse of the plains, the depths of the lingering light, the distance from me to the horizon and beyond it, it was all that voice saying good afternoon and looking at me, it was all his face. I followed the long road back to town and reached home just as night was falling. In the yard I would find my mother where I'd left her. During the day she had built a high tower, or a tree with all its leaves, or another of those faces that were always of the same person but that sometimes smiled and at other times cried, that were sometimes full of life and joy, at other times dead and with the invariable expression of eternal sadness. In those first days, because the house needed it, I went there every day. And before falling asleep, beyond the incoherent words my mother uttered in the silence, I saw nothing but José arriving from the fields and looking at me, looking at me, seeing that I looked at him, we looked at each other.

· · ·

FOR THOSE WITH UNDERSTANDING, this heat is gloomy. This ardent sun is a deathly caress on the skin. This light is life itself, burning up. For those with understanding, this long summer is black: black behind the light, black behind the sun, black beneath the heat. And it's in this summer that she comes, walking along the road with a listless, ever so tired step. The imposition of living obliges her to walk, to keep going, stopping in the few patches of shade along the road; and all the heat, all the light, is a gloomy shade. And sadness is her gaze while she walks the road, her eyes staring at the ground. Sadness will be her gaze when she appears at the gate to the farmstead. Carrying a heavy and painful death, she'll walk without stopping over the land, in the afternoon, inside the light, straight to the rich people's house. She won't see me, even as she won't see the silence of the mallows that she passes. And time, wearing her down, will continue. When she leaves, a little before José pens up the sheep or a little after José enters the house, she'll look at me with a sorrowful gaze, and since she knows I'll go visit her mother tomorrow, she'll say see you tomorrow.

But today she won't need to choose a moment among possible moments, because today José didn't go to the fields. I took some hay to the sheep and changed their water. The window of José's bedroom has been closed all day. In the air there's a faraway peacefulness, the size of a whole man. Tattered clouds slowly glide by. The light makes all things glow, including all the animals' gazes and all the trees' leaves and all the stones. I'm old and I know. This sun shows us more clearly the ruins. What we see is what has remained. We are granted our heart's desire only for it to be definitively taken away, since our dream of it perishes. This sun shows us our own desperateness. For those with understanding, this sun is the hand that caresses us and crushes us.

This sun is the lullaby sung by our mother to put us to sleep, and it wakes us up in the unbearable darkness of our no longer having a mother and finding ourselves in this sweltering and hopeless solitude. For those with understanding, this summer is black. For those with understanding, this heat is gloomy.

AFTER SALOMÃO VANISHED DOWN THE PATH leading him home, after the first sounds of night arrived, José returned with the flock of sheep. The animals' short legs could be heard stumbling on the stones, their quick steps sounding like a sack of small potatoes poured onto a table. The night was a languid melancholy, a veil of black marble surrounding the fields and weighing inside José. He unraveled the wires on the gate and waited for the sheep to enter. His motions were absent, unrecorded in memory. José's eyes were large. The old, old sheepdog withdrew. The stars and the unattainable peace of the cicadas could be heard in the distance. José went around the sheep pen to behind the feed troughs, where he leaned his staff, hung up his shoulder bag on a nail, and took off his black sheepskin and his shirt. And he remembered all of Salomão's words. Is it true, José? His ingenuous voice and words. It's not true, is it? His cousin's face and José's sincere regret, those words and José's remorse spreading across the whole plain and the world as he knew it. I know it can't be true. Naked from the waist up, his eyes were larger than night, and all the stars were mirrored in his gaze. He grabbed the rope that hung on a gatepost and swung it in an arc across his left shoulder. First the rope traced dark streaks on his back where tiny red beads appeared; then blood began to flow in vertical lines, alternating with the rope's steady beating; finally his back was a single curtain of blood, which spattered each time the rope struck. José kept his eyes wide open. His powerful arm did not relent. The rope slashed the air with a groan and cracked against his back. José switched hands and continued until his hands trembled. He set down the rope. Buttoning all its buttons, he put his shirt back on over the blood. He donned his black sheepskin. He went into the house. He walked past his mother sitting by the fire and they didn't talk. Lying on the bed in his bedroom, in the darkness, José looked at the ceiling and at all the sun that he knew.

T HE APPRENTICE LEFT, SA-
lomão left, and Master Rafael kept running the plane across the
board that was to become a doorframe. He wielded the plane
with his only hand, making the board perfectly smooth. Even
when the days grew longer, Master Rafael always worked until
the last ray of sunlight, and on that afternoon he was so lost in
his own thoughts that he didn't hear Salomão say see you tomorrow, nor did he hear the apprentice ask can I leave now, my
mother's waiting for me to milk the goats?, nor did he hear himself say okay, you can go. And when, in a pause between two
memories, he woke up and realized he was alone, he smiled at
his discovery and went over to the window. It was a wide window,

its panes covered with sawdust, and it was open. He steadied himself on the sill, and with his only eye and his only ear he drank up the sunset's luminosity and its symphony of sounds. The lumberyard had no fence, and the landscape stretched across the properties of Doctor Mateus, across a gentle wheat field that ended in a golden summit where the sun disappeared among the stalks of grain. A balmy breeze rose up out of the heat, and it was like a fresh breath expanding in waves over the wheat, as when a stone is tossed into a pool of water. The vast unbounded skies converged on the place where the smoldering sun was setting, as if they also wished to sink out of sight, letting the night prevail. In a dense mixture of opposing movements, like a sheet of bodies shaken in a whirlwind, the sparrows went around in a burst of cheeps, making the most of the day's last meanders. Dusk. And Master Rafael, within himself, was larger. He thought of the blind prostitute. In that moment the whole surface of the sky was but one of her gestures; the sun's nimbus glowing on the earth's horizon was but a strand of her hair; the thousand-voiced melody of the sparrows was but the beginning of one of her sighs; the infinite expanse of the plain was but the soft skin on the tip of one of her fingers. He thought, and his thoughts seemed truer to him than thoughts, for he knew that he would go visit her that evening. Slowly night touched the earth, and only then did Master Rafael go on his way. Supporting himself on his crutch, he closed the windows and closed the doors. His father had made the crutch one week before he died. It was light, strong, and did not hurt his armpit. It had replaced another, smaller one, which had replaced another, smaller one, which had replaced another, smaller one. But now Master Rafael was a man and would grow no more, and when sometimes he sat down and looked at it, that

crutch seemed to him more durable than eternal things, such
was the care that had gone into its making and such the apprecia-
tion he'd felt for it over the years. He closed the gate, slamming it
with a thunderous clang. He walked home, accompanied only by
the repeated sound of the crutch stabbing the ground and by the
voices of people on their doorsteps greeting him. He passed by
Salomão's house, which was next to the house of the man shut
up in a room writing, and as always happened, upon hearing the
sound of the crutch, still coated with shavings and sawdust, Salomão came outside and said see you tomorrow. Master Rafael
raised his gaze a little and kept going. When he reached his door
he opened it, closed it, and did not light the kerosene lamp. He
knew where everything was. He grabbed a piece of hard bread
and, as if it were cork, used a knife to cut it up into slices over a
bowl. Since he had half a coffeepot left over from breakfast, he
poured the cold coffee over the bread, sat down at the table, and
swallowed large spoonfuls of bread and coffee. Then he lifted the
bowl to his mouth and sipped the crumb-filled liquid, which for
him was the best part. He paused for a moment, feeling satisfied,
then burped and stood up. He filled the washbasin. It was a washbasin made of painted iron, with an enamel jug underneath,
a small mirror on top, the basin itself in the middle, a place for
soap, and a short iron bar on which to hang a towel. He took off
all his clothes and draped them over the chair in his bedroom. He
returned to the kitchen, and in the darkness, in front of the washbasin, he washed his arm to the elbow and washed his face and
neck, working up a good lather. Clean and fresh, back in his bedroom, he put on the clothes that, summer or winter, he always
wore on nights when he visited the blind prostitute: a pair of
brown trousers, with the right leg folded and secured with safety

pins, a white shirt and a gray jacket, with the right sleeves folded and secured with safety pins. He ran his fingers through his hair, undoing the shape made by his cap, and left.

I WALKED IN THE NIGHT. What led me to her wasn't the streets. My foot and crutch trampled the parched earth and dust, but that wasn't me, and I went forward in the night. And what I'm now calling night was a cool, black, and necessary silence, which wrapped me, and I perhaps floated. What led me wasn't the streets. And yet, if I search my memory, I know I'll find those streets that go from my house to hers, I know I'll find people's faces seeing me well dressed and saying good evening with a smile that wanted to say other things, I know I'll remember the stars vaguely shining overhead. And all of this which I didn't notice but which reached me like a forgotten remembrance, told by someone who assures me it was so, happened before the only thing that truly happened on that night, or in my life. And all that time from before seems to have lost its meaning. I lived inside a cloud during that time. Inside a cloud I learned the faded colors of the fog, and I believed that the earth was dull brown, that the grass was dull green, that the light didn't exist. And in those final moments of that time before, ignorant and blind, I walked in the night. I climbed the last steps of the night. Almost there. Without realizing it. Before.

HE KNOCKED ON THE DOOR VERY LIGHTLY. He tapped the door very lightly with his knuckles. He let only the sound of his knuckles touch the door. The blind prostitute's footsteps made no sound. The door opened. He reached for her face, but she was already retreating to the dim light of the kitchen. Her slender body was a shadow in the light of the lamp she'd lit for his sake. The blind prostitute was no more than thirty-some years old. People said she was the great-great-granddaughter of a baroness. Everyone had heard it from someone who had heard it from someone. What was known for certain is that she'd inherited her blindness and profession from her mother, who'd inherited them from her grandmother, who'd inherited them from her great-grandmother. Ten years ago the blind prostitute had a sad and honest, innocent-looking face. On the day her mother died, ten years ago, she didn't cry. On that day, for the first time, she stuck her fingers into the cavities of her eyes and tried to discover what it meant to see, what it meant to cry. On that day, now buried under ten years of mourning, she felt relieved as her mother weakly breathed her last, and then she felt a great confusion in her hands, which groped at the walls as she walked about lost in the house she'd always known. And on that day, ten years ago, not a week had gone by since the morning when her mother had woken up with the old scars on her back and belly oozing tiny beads of blood, the morning when her mother got up and said get my bed ready for me to die. And with anxious haste, full of fear, the daughter cleaned the blood from her scars with towels, and new beads of fresh blood replaced the old ones in the very same places. The nights passed. The scars opened slowly, like brand-new sores. The amount of blood increased. And the daughter placed towels over the wounds, removing them only when she began to feel the warmth of the blood on her hands. No one came to visit them that week. On the night before she died, the mother mustered all her strength to run the palms of her hands over her daughter's face, slowly, to see her. In the bedroom there was dried blood on the walls and floor, and the whole room smelled of blood. Blood was flowing from the mother's skin like a raging river when it suddenly stopped. The daughter said nothing for a moment. Her mother stopped breathing. Master Rafael closed the front door and followed her to the bedroom. Ten years ago the blind prostitute's mother had died in that bed, cold and pale, without a drop of blood left in her body.

First she, then he, sat down on the bed. The only light was what came in from the kitchen. Master Rafael didn't need to see her to understand she had some news to share. She directed her missing eyes to a place where there was nothing and no one. The bedroom smelled stuffy, embarrassed. He placed his hand in her hands and understood from their hesitant and warm grasp, without a word spoken, that something would unite them forever. And all eternity, all silence, hinged on that moment. And when she took Master Rafael's hand and placed it on the clothes covering her belly, his lips broke into what was perhaps a smile, and his enormous gaze looked for her. She wasn't smiling. Only when he, in a child's voice, said we're going to get married, did her grave but serene expression soften into a gentle nod of simple, sheer joy.

I WALKED IN THE NIGHT. Returning home, imagining what it would be like to walk those streets with the certainty that she'd be waiting for me, I walked in the night. Imagining everything the same, the town fast asleep, the coolness, the calm, but with a profound and natural certainty. That was how I saw the life of married men. An additional certainty, strong and steady. A certainty. She would wait for me, my wife would wait for me, and the little boy would be sleeping, my son would be sleeping. I'd walk in the night, armed with this certainty. And as I crossed the town's peacefulness, all the sounds, the crickets, the crescent moon, the barking dogs, the dogs answering each other from one side of town to the other, the dogs howling, it was all absolutely external to me, it was all a distant, perhaps impossible reality, beyond my skin and my gaze. But when I passed by the tiny fountain at the beginning of Salomão's street, the sound of the water trickling from the spout and falling on the stone entered the night that was in me and made me stop. Leaning against a wall, I heard, in a blend of voices and memories, women talking and men shouting from afar and children singing an endless refrain; I heard lame, I heard cripple, I heard half a man. I heard or remembered. I tried to forget. I leaned once more on my crutch and went on, fooling myself, thinking how little their talk mattered, how it was nothing, how it would all end on the day I married her, on the day our son was born. I broke the silence to open the door to my house and, closing it, I returned the house and the world to silence. Slowly. The vast darkness. I sat on a chair and greatly wished my father were alive. Dad, I'm going to get married. Dad, I'm going to have a son, you're going to have a grandson. Dad, I'm happy.

THE KITCHEN, BESIDES ITS DOORS, had a single small window looking out onto the backyard. When morning arrived with its sounds and bustle and growing light, it entered by that window. Master Rafael was still in the chair where he'd sat down after arriving home from the blind prostitute's house. And the square of light that came through the window spread across the floor in a long rectangle that touched the foot of Master Rafael, climbing up his leg and torso to his face. His gaze was that of someone who'd thought of many things. Cracking the joints of his knee and his spine, he stood up. In his bedroom he got dressed for work. He didn't light the stove, he drank no coffee, and he went out. Outside he felt as if the dawn were greeting him. In the morning clarity, the whitewashed walls were brighter, the earth and dust and stones cooler. Torpid, half-asleep dogs eyed Master Rafael. Swallows flew close to the ground, like harmless volleys from a slingshot. Putting his weight on the wooden crutch, then on his one leg, his staggered way of walking seemed steadier and surer to him that morning. When he reached the carpenter's shop there was a glow over the roof and over the yard that he didn't notice. No one was waiting for him at the gate. He was the first to arrive. He walked through the shavings and sawdust, between the table and the benches, and opened the window. The air was fresh, his breathing fresh. And for the first time a voice inside him spoke up and said she bestows her favors on lots of men, how can I be sure the child is mine? And immediately, without an intervening second, he felt ashamed for having doubted. He went to the bench and took up the plane. The boards of the doorframe he was making were where he had left them the previous evening, but with more time, with a layer of time on them, like a layer of dust. He began planing them. A short while later the apprentice arrived. Good morning. Then Salomão.

The apprentice spent the whole morning cleaning up. He gathered wood scraps from the floor and threw them on a pile in the yard, and with a wooden scoop he transferred little mounds of sawdust and shavings onto a large cloth, whose four corners he then joined in his right hand, carrying the cloth on his back to the largest pile in the yard: a small sawdust mountain. Nearly every day someone would show up with an empty sack, wanting to fill it with shavings to make a bed for rabbits in a rabbit hutch. Every week the baker would come by with his pushcart to take away wood scraps and boards that were of no use for carpentry work but were excellent for burning in his bread oven. But no one could make use of the whole pile of scraps or the whole pile of sawdust, so busy was the shop, and the piles were rising into the sky. Master Rafael and Salomão were in the yard. The apprentice went back and forth behind them, briskly when carrying a load, slowly after dumping it. The sun was hot, as if it were afternoon, and a glowing mist rose up from the ground covered with pinewood chips, a mist like the sound of burning, like water, like half-transparent, half-frosted glass. Master Rafael held his end of the saw, and he had more power in that one hand than most men have in two. On the other side of the log that they were cutting, Salomão, with sweat running down his face, signaled that he needed some water. He tilted the earthen jug until the bowl was filled, and drank voraciously while Master Rafael slowly walked over. Then he bent down again, refilled the bowl, and handed it to Master Rafael, who took it and said I want to tell you something. And he lifted the bowl to his lips, covering his whole face up to his blind eye and the eye that looked straight at Salomão. The gazes of both men were linked for a moment. Taking the bowl from his mouth, he shook out the remaining drops of water, slung it over the neck of the jug, stood up straight, and said I'm going to marry the blind prostitute. Salomão smiled like a young boy, put his hand on the master's shoulder, and congratulated him. Master Rafael also smiled.

ONIGHT MY BODY DIDN'T ASK
for sleep. I lay down in bed, but my eyes didn't close. I remained
in the light, which filled me up: a light from the sky, from the
sun, breaking through the night and the roof and my chest, a
light blinding me to everything else. I lay there with my legs extended and with my arms extended but without feeling them. I
think: perhaps pain exists to forewarn us of a yet greater suffering. On my back, beneath my clothing, I feel the pain of raw
flesh. I think: pain exists to forewarn us of a greater pain. And all
day and all night my mother sat, she still sits, next to the fire. As
if it were cold, as if she lived in a never-ending winter, she sits
very still next to the embers, with the flames lighting up her face

and reveries. And sometimes she stirs the embers with the tongs, or quickens them with the fan. Sometimes she moves a pot closer to the fire, or puts a pot on the trivet. Sometimes she gets up and fetches more wood: brushwood, sticks, logs: wood that she brings back all hunched over, very quickly, so as not to be away from the fire for more than a deep breath. And she sits there, withdrawn into a nocturnal mourning, hypnotized, as if her small and frail body were absorbing all the fire, as if she lived in a never-ending winter, as if it were cold. And outside, beyond the house walls, the sun burns, as it burns here in my silence. The sun ruthlessly withers the grass, our skin, our hopes. And yet you know I understand you, mother. Even if I don't say it. Even if you don't say it. You know that when I walk past you and you look at me with pleading in your gaze, I feel like caressing you, I feel like holding your hands the way I did when you took me into your arms and were so much my mother, the way I did when I was a little boy. But today, when I walk past you, I'm no longer the boy you called to yourself with open arms. Today, a man and indifferent, I walk past you and pretend not to hear the laments in your gaze. And yet you know I understand you. I understand your freezing cold in the middle of August, your mourning that makes you weak, weak, weak. As I understood you on the night when I was getting ready to go meet her in town, and you looked at me and said without words don't go. I understood you on that night when she was waiting for me, when the excitement in my blood suddenly halted, and I listened to you, let my hands fall, and entered this solitary bedroom and lay down on this solitary bed where I am right now, alone. Mother, you sit by the fire and shiver with cold, the way burning embers gelidly shiver, and there in the distance where you are the night's mirror, you know that I've never hated you. I'm your son and your reflection. And outside the yard is now golden with the light of the sunset, and she walks across that light. Abandoned, with a scarf on her head and looking down, she has stopped questioning the world. Old Gabriel says to her see you tomorrow. Soon the lingering light will lie down in its black coffin. And here I remain in a seemingly endless midday, wrapped all around by an impenetrable solitude.

WHEN OLD GABRIEL SAID SEE YOU TOMORROW, I was an almost invisible piece of the afternoon touching him. I kept walking, leaving him yet farther behind me. The path cutting through the plains brought me to where I am now. On the road back to town, walking. Already far from the Mount of Olives but still close to the long afternoon I spent at the rich people's house. And here I cross paths with myself going to the farmstead after lunch. I see myself coming my way. It's me going to the farmstead. And I'm coming from the farmstead. I'm coming from the farmstead and see myself going to the farmstead. I'm going to the farmstead and remember the face of Salomão eating and smiling for no reason; I remember Salomão asking me for a needle, raising one of his rough hands up to the light and, with the tip of the needle, digging into his finger's skin to extract a pinewood splinter. That's what Salomão did during lunch and that's what I thought about. I pass by myself. I pass by these thoughts. The sun's scorching heat makes me sweat. I was walking in the hottest hour. When I reach the rich people's house, I'll dust and sweep and open the windows of the upstairs bedrooms, and then I'll sit in the main hallway, in front of the voice shut up inside a trunk. That's what I did. I pass by myself. I pass by these thoughts. I tidied up the house in half an hour and spent the rest of the afternoon listening to the voice shut up inside a trunk. I heard it say many things, but I paid the most attention when it said: pain exists to forewarn us of a yet greater suffering. I heard the voice shut up inside a trunk say these words, and I see myself vanish down the road, heading toward the Mount of Olives to hear them for the first time. Here, where I'm walking, the sun slowly declines. I keep on. The town awaits me, with its streets and the women whispering as I pass by. My mother awaits me, without knowing it. In the evening I'll hear her talk to herself, repeating her eternal story. Her oppressively eternal story, not because it never ends but because it never lets up, because there's no pause to distinguish the end from the beginning. In the evening I'll do nothing but hear her, like on that night when I didn't sleep and the next day the doors and windows of José's house were all shut, as they also were today. It happened in the April when I started working at the rich people's house. On that late afternoon, balmy like this one, José arrived from the fields when I was leaving. We stopped and looked at each other. He said good afternoon, and his voice was part of that soft light. In the sky above us a stork glided by very slowly, its wings wide open, carrying a dry stick in its very long beak. And that moment was ours and enormous. Looking at me steadily, he said wait for me, tonight I'll come and fetch you. And on that day I didn't feel the long walk to town as I feel it today, every single step. I arrived home, brought my mother inside, and gathered some clothes into a bundle. It was already dark, I was folding a shirt, when through the wall I thought I heard the man shut up in a windowless room writing begin to cry. The never-ending stream of his fountain pen paused for longer than usual, and I thought I heard two teardrops fall on the tabletop. Perhaps they're two drops of ink, I thought. In the kitchen I heated up some water to make bread soup and gave it to my mother. With each spoonful the imagined face of José appeared more distinctly in the real space of the doorway. Looking at what I was thinking, I sometimes missed my mother's mouth, and I'd see him, I'd hear him say come with me. That night, when I removed the bib from her neck, it was dirtier than usual, spotted with dried broth. I looked intently at my mother and smiled, trying to tell her my joy. I took her to the stool by the stove, straightened her clothes, and combed her hair with my fingers. I sat down. I placed my hands on my legs. And we waited. And we waited. Which made the time drag even more. That night each minute was like a whole night. A breeze that came and went kept making the door shake and I quivered within. And time, its substance, entered slowly, very slowly, through my pores. He's sure to come, he's on his way and is sure to come. And time. My mother repeated the words she repeated and repeated, she repeated her gazing and her breathing, her gazing and her breathing, the avid breathing between her words, her gazing, she repeated, she repeated her own self until she was many, all the same, in the same place, in a repeated time. And I looked at my hands, not believing that they were empty, not believing that I could ever imagine them as anything but empty. And the kerosene lamp made us older. The feeble, doomed shadows bowed down and slowly advanced, like smoke, along the floor and the walls. He's sure to come, he's on his way and is sure to come. And when it was probably already very late my mother's breathing became longer, her words occupied her breath. Her chin had fallen against her chest. She slept. I took her to the bedroom and laid her in bed. I took off her slippers, took off her clothes, and covered her with the sheets. I caressed her cheeks. I would have liked him to see her, I would have liked to show him my mother, I would have liked to say to him this is my mother. And her skin, peaceful and distant, so calm under my

fingers. I slowly closed the door. I blew out the lamp. I sat down.
I rested my hands on my legs. Alone, in the darkness, I waited
until the first light of morning.

DON'T GO. AND I DIDN'T GO. Even though I'd waited all day,
all my life, for that moment, unique among all moments, even
though I'd imagined in detail the world just beyond the bound-
ary of that moment, I didn't go. Don't go. Even though a stork
rose up in flight, gliding like an embrace we've never known but
imagine to be possible, even though I looked at her with my
whole being, even though I said wait for me, tonight I'll come
and fetch you, even though the twilight had seen us where only
sincere souls go, I came into this room, lay down on this bed, let
that unique moment pass by indistinctly and let my life become a
painful place of squandered moments, moments squandered before their time, during the weariness of their time, after the bad
memory of their time, in the tedium of having and expecting
nothing. Don't go. And I didn't go. You didn't lose me, mother.
I lost myself. I failed to find myself where I'd never been, where
I'll never be. And I don't blame you at all, as I don't blame the
moon that rises every night, or the sun, or the earth that pulls
me. I don't blame you at all. And now that I know where you
are, you who always seemed forgotten over there, you whom I
always saw forgotten amid the ruins of a muffled silence, amid
what men one day named death, amid what men one day named
night and cold; now that I know where you are, I have to get up
from this bed. It's already very late, darkness has covered the
fields, and the plains are nothing but darkness: the screeching
of bats, the owls' whooping, the crickets, and the world's vast
silence. I have to get up from this bed. I slowly close my eyelids
to this sun I see in front of me, this sun that enters me not to

cleanse me of shadows but to suffocate me. I slowly open my eyelids, and in this room's darkness I begin to see this body, perfectly still, which doesn't seem mine. I slowly take possession of it: first the arms, which I raise, then my legs, and I sit up in bed. I'm myself again. I need to wash and put on clean clothes. I remove my trousers from my ridiculously thin legs. I start to remove my shirt, and it's stuck to the dried blood on my back; I work it loose from bottom to top, and it's a membrane that pulls off scabs stuck to the fabric. I think: pain exists to forewarn us of a yet greater suffering. I put on clean socks. I clean off my back with a towel. I put on a white undershirt, a clean shirt, clean trousers. I don't put on my cap. I go to the kitchen. Dry logs crackle in the fire, and its dying light is the only light. My mother's body is dark; only her old and sad face glows. I walk across her gaze. I open and close the outside door. The night is how I know it: deep and black, wrapping me in itself and telling me that I'm the same night that the night is. I don't stick my hands in my pockets, I let them and my arms hang free. I lift my eyes and gaze at the night in the sky, not the stars but the black space that separates them.

I REMEMBER, AND I STILL FEEL in my hands, that dawn, that slow light. And everything was cruel because everything was like it was on other days, because there was nothing that took pity, because time was passing through the world, or the world though time, and I, a particle, a tiny bit of the world, couldn't stop it. Dawn. The first sounds of dawn. Birds. The first wave of people going by outside. And my mother's voice. My mother repeating the same words, the same words, the same words. Me having to get up. Feeling each of my movements to be isolated from the ones before and the ones after it, and each fraction of each movement harsh and cruel, each millimeter against me. In the bedroom, my mother's eyes. I got her dressed. I gave her some coffee. And when I took her into the yard, the dawn was already a new morning. And I still feel in my hands the warm breeze, warming up slowly, warming up until it was a bellows blowing a fiery breath. Like the breeze that arrives here from the town and touches my face and neck, and tries to hold me here so that I'll never reach the town and it will never be night. Like the poppies, here amid the flames of the wheat fields, like still-brighter and hotter embers. And then, when the days stopped being different from each other, when the walk to the Mount of Olives became longer, when I stopped seeing José, when I began to leave a little bit earlier to avoid meeting José, when the days all blended into a single day that's all days, then old Gabriel knocked on my door and, before sitting down next to my mother in the yard, said I've brought someone who wants to meet you. And the frightened face of Salomão appeared, very faintly, on the threshold. Old Gabriel told him to sit down, pulled over a chair for him, pulled over a chair for me, and went out into the yard. I joined my hands together like a little girl, I joined my feet together, and looked at the floor, without seeing the floor, focusing only on the edges of my gaze and on the silence. He also sat still, shifting now and then only to get comfortable in the uncomfortable chair, and he never stopped looking at me, with a rat's eyes, as if he were examining a fearful object. We sat there like that for two hours, face-to-face without talking, just feeling each other's presence, intimidated by each other's presence. And when old Gabriel returned, he also stopped to look at us, perhaps smiling, and to Salomão he said shall we get going?, and Salomão said hmm, or said uh-huh, and suddenly stood up. Before they left, old Gabriel said see you tomorrow. Salomão didn't say anything.

And the next day, or two days later, Salomão's mother showed up. She knocked on the door and entered. She walked past me, sat down, and began to talk very fast. She said her son wanted to marry me, and she said we'd get married in three weeks, and she said our courtship would take place at her house, every other day and always in her presence, as she didn't want any hanky-panky, and she said our courtship would begin the next day, as there was no time to lose, and she said to show up in the early evening, and she said she liked trimmed nails and scrubbed necks. She said she admired how I'd raised myself, and she said it was her idea for her son to marry me, and she said her son needed the care of a kind wife, and she said I'd be a good match for him. She said that he'd greatly disappointed her by refusing to work with his father, and she said that his father was a horseshoer but that he, Salomão, had always been afraid of animals. She said his father had died from a kick in the head by a mule he was shoeing, and that much I already knew, and she said she'd gotten a job for Salomão at Master Rafael's carpentry shop, where he still worked. She said she was all alone. I didn't say anything. She stood up, said good day, and left because she had things to do. And so for three weeks, every other day, in the early evening, Salomão and I had our courtship. We sat next to each other in separate chairs, and his mother sat opposite, knitting a little jacket for the son she said we were going to have in two years' time. He looked at me dumbfounded, I looked at the floor, and his mother talked. She told stories of when Salomão was little and was afraid of heights, of the dark, of mice, of spiders, of lizards, of grasshoppers, of crickets, of centipedes, of flying ants. And three weeks later I got married. I don't know on what date, and I don't feel like figuring out in which month, but I know it was a Sunday. I took my mother by the arm to the church. Going on foot through the

sun-battered streets, I in a wedding dress lent to me by Salomão's
mother, we got there on time. The devil was already at the altar.
The others were late. José, Salomão's cousin, didn't come because their mothers didn't get along. The others were late, but
they got there. Salomão's mother pulled her son by the arm as if
she'd dragged him there by force. Almost purple, she wore a very
tight dress, an imitation-pearl necklace that dug into her neck,
and a nosegay of plastic tulips on her head. The devil began, and
the words he said in the tiny space of the church, spoken as if he
were uttering them from the pulpit of the world, blended with
his smile. And when the devil was about to ask for our yeses, Salomão's mother fell to the floor. Dead. Wide-eyed, asphyxiated,
choked by her dress and necklace and weighed down by the
tulips. And the devil quickly asked us the question, we said yes
yes, and only then turned our attention to the deceased. So it was
a mixture of wedding and funeral, for as soon as we answered
the question, they carried Salomão's mother on a pew over to the
altar, and the devil, with his lips pressed in a kind of smile, said
some words on her behalf. On exiting from the church, we were
greeted by a funeral wagon with a coffin, as one of the guests, and
the guests were all her neighbors, had got out the word. They
laid Salomão's mother in the coffin and shut the lid. Though no
one was especially grieved, we made the trip to the cemetery in
silence and at the speed of a religious procession. I left my bridal
wreath on her coffin, and those were the only flowers she had.
With my mother on one side and Salomão on the other, we returned to the town. By the time we reached his street, the hem
of my dress was black from having trailed it in dirt and dust. He
opened the door, we went in, and there was a large table full
of food in the living room. Famished, we took three plates and
helped ourselves. He waited for me to feed my mother, and then

we had lunch together. For a month we ate codfish croquettes and coconut balls wrapped in collared paper. The sugar cookies and lard cakes lasted almost a year. Today I still remember all of this vividly, but I know that one day, looking back, I'll remember none of it. What I'll never forget, after no matter how many years and deaths, is that endless night, moment by moment, like a night that was an ocean, and I a pebble at the very bottom, never touched by the light. And I arrive home precisely when the afternoon ends. Salomão has still not arrived. I go to the yard and bring my mother into the kitchen. I go back to the yard by myself. I lift my eyes and gaze at the night in the sky, not the stars but the black space that separates them.

IT WAS SATURDAY. NO ONE would dare say it, but the sun was gentler, the chickens walked more briskly on the streets, the pigeons made wider circles in the sky. The women were all carrying bags of bread and stopped to talk with one another. The men's faces were all washed. Basking in the morning, the grass gladly waved. It was Saturday. Master Rafael had been at the blind prostitute's house since the first colors of dawn. Salomão and the apprentice arrived at the hour when they usually began at the carpenter's shop. It was the third and last Saturday they spent renovating the house. On the first Saturday, with three picks and three shovels, they dug a cesspool some twenty feet deep in the backyard, and by the time night arrived they had already made a cover so solid that the earth overlaying it would never cave in, even if they planted a ninety-year-old cork tree on top of it. On the second Saturday, they installed the toilet in a corner of the kitchen and connected the drainpipe to the cesspool. It was a lighter day of work, and Master Rafael, who hadn't had time the week before to plot his ambitions, spent the day making plans. I'll build a china cabinet to go here, I'll make some shelves for over there. And at lunchtime, while they waited for the blind prostitute to arrive with three bowls of bread soup, each with a special treat of two grilled sardines, Master Rafael took the pencil from his ear, a small and thin sheet of wood from his pocket, and began to draw detailed plans for making the most of the area in the yard: lemon trees grafted into orange trees, apricot trees grafted into peach trees, grapevines, cabbages, flower beds with colorful patterns, lilies, mallows, and invented plants. Another show of his enthusiasm was when, at the end of the day, he asked his employees to wait in the yard while he tried out the toilet. Salomão and the apprentice stood there in silence, hands in their pockets, listening to the sounds in the kitchen, increased by the toilet's flushing, and with greater attention they heard the water and filth passing through the drainpipe. Master Rafael, with his belt still unbuckled, jumped up and down on his crutch. The blind prostitute arrived right behind him with three glasses and a bottle of red wine. Now, on the third Saturday, they were going to install two windows, one in the bedroom wall next to the backyard, and another in the kitchen wall facing onto the street. They began with the bedroom window. Master Rafael measured it, outlined it with a pencil on the whitewash, and began to hammer out the wall with his one and only hand. The hammer had a handle the size of a man's arm, and the hammer's head was made of a special steel, with a special alloy that had been a generations-old secret but was forever lost when an identical hammer hit the head of the blacksmith's youngest son, crushing it instantaneously. Even though the hammer was heavier than a woman, Master Rafael grabbed it by the tip of the handle, twirled it, and made it strike exactly where he wanted, with a bang that came from the depths of the earth or of men or of who knows what. In the yard the apprentice sifted spadefuls of sand, and with a hoe Salomão mixed the sand with cement and water into a coherent but not stiff mixture, soft but not runny. When Master Rafael had finished opening the hole, Salomão went to the toolbox to fetch a chisel and a carpenter's hammer and made the oval hole into a rectangular shape. Even though the bed was covered with a drop cloth and plaster dust, the bedroom looked like a happy place for the first time; the light discovered its every nook, chasing out the gloom of many generations. The apprentice fetched the varnished window that Master Rafael had made on three late afternoons, and after driving large nails in crosswise around the edges, they began to secure it with trowels full of cement. Salomão, with hammer in hand, went to the kitchen to start the next window. Its shape was already outlined on the wall. Using both hands, Salomão slammed the hammer into the rectangular area, and the bricks didn't budge, as the wall was very thick. On his second try, the first rubble gave way. A ray of sunlight shot through the wall. And Salomão, peeking through the hole, saw the devil on the other side. As if he'd known that Salomão was going to open a window there, as if he'd been waiting for him. The devil was on the street, a foot away from the wall, looking at him, smiling.

AS I SAT DOWN under the big old cork tree and the sheep, knowing we'd arrived, scattered across the pasture, I remembered Salomão's voice. When we were kids I was already bringing the sheep here, and sometimes, when the sun was at its hottest, he would show up by himself, having escaped his mother, so that for an afternoon he ran free with me. We'd catch crickets. I taught him to distinguish between male and female crickets by the number of tails, and I said don't ever take a female cricket home, because they attract snakes. He was scared to death of snakes, but my warning was useless, because he was just as scared of crickets, male or female. He would never touch one, and to take one home was unthinkable. We'd gather acorns. I taught him the difference between those from cork trees and those from oak trees, explaining that the latter were very bitter and could only be eaten by boars. He nodded and said yes, as if he'd understood, and then he ate both kinds of acorns, with his same rabbit's teeth and his same naïve and childish expression. At day's end, we'd sit and look at the sheep, as if looking at a stream, while I chewed on a stalk of sorrel. And each time I yanked a stalk for him, he shook his head as if I'd offered him a red-hot iron. He said that sorrel was bitter and that his mother had told him it was poisonous. Offended, I wouldn't look at him, and in a harsh voice I'd say good, that leaves more for me, as if it were almost gone, as if the fields around us weren't full of those tiny yellow flowers.

But the truth that at the time I wouldn't even confess to myself was that those afternoons filled me with excitement. Neither I nor Salomão played with other children. I didn't play with other children because there weren't any at the farmstead, and I never went into town except with my mother to visit the cemetery. He didn't play with the other children in the town because his mother wouldn't let him and because the only time he snuck out to play with them, they played a trick on him with nettles: they surrounded him, took off his long johns, and covered him with nettles, and for a week he had to douse his privates with vinegar to relieve the itching and burning. We only played with each other. And we never lost the excitement we shared, I in secret, he without knowing how to hide it. Although I realized that those afternoons were now impossible, I still felt that excitement the last time I saw him, beneath all my sorrow and regret. A repressed, unspoken excitement, sunny like on those distant afternoons, black like on my afternoons today. And I feel like shouting Salomão, Salomão, the way I used to shout, seeing him turn around with his dependable smile. I miss him and I know we can never play again. And all I'd like to do is play. All I'd like is to take him through the fields and explain things to him, while the sheepdog wags her tail, because he's my cousin and my friend. I feel like shouting Salomão, Salomão, but this has also become impossible, like the earth, like the sun. And those afternoons, so long and so special, are now long and make me die over and over, moment by moment. Like me, my staff leans against the trunk of the big old cork tree. Dropping my jackknife from one hand and the branch I was whittling from the other hand, I look straight at the sun. I think: if the punishment that's my lot can be contained in me, if I can accept it and somehow hold it inside me, perhaps I'll be spared further judgments, perhaps I can rest. And all the trees between me and the sky suddenly disappeared, so that it looked perfectly clear and distant. And the sun's burning slowed into a steady, dull heat. And the world's voices: the voices of stones, breezes, trees: all the world's voices fell silent. And where the earth ends in my field of vision, I see a figure slowly take shape. It's a very large man, walking toward me. He's a man the size of a house or a haystack. He's a very large man, looking straight at me and walking very fast. And like a galloping breeze, he's already near me. He stops. I make out his face. He looks at me. We look at each other. I can't bear the force of his enormous gaze and instantly, instinctively, turn my head away. Slowly turning back to look, I see he has disappeared. In his place there's just the swift flight of birds under the sun's flames, just the agony of the stones and the burning breeze and the trees enduring the day's fire. I stand up, stick my fingers in the corners of my mouth, press them against my folded tongue, whistle, and say come on dog, and I whistle again. I've got to go see Salomão. The sheepdog rounds up the flock, running on both sides of it at the same time. I've got to go see Salomão. On the way to the Mount of Olives, I prod the lagging sheep with my staff. I've got to go see Salomão.

THE HAMMER IN SALOMÃO'S HAND began to tremble. On the street the devil, almost leaning against the wall, kept smiling. And Salomão struck the wall with the hammer half a dozen times, since that was how many times it took to make the right-sized hole for the window. And not one piece of rubble hit the devil, nor did one speck of dust disrupt the perfect harmony of his clean shirt, his pleated trousers, and his smile. Standing there balancing the hammer, with his left hand grasping the handle and his right hand near the head, Salomão gazed at the devil. With the visor of his cap sticking out from between the dull tips of his horns, casting a shadow so small it didn't cover his eyes, the devil smiled and gazed at Salomão. And everything he said, and that Salomão understood, wasn't in words. Everything he said was in that steady gaze, in that tempting smile. That fixed gaze full of hazy shapes, ripping through Salomão and rummaging inside him. That smile telling him, through vaguely curved lips, through an imperceptible and obvious grimace, your wife is cheating on you; when you look and think you know what she's thinking, you don't know what she's thinking, you don't know who you're looking at; your wife is cheating on you and you're alone, deceived, and everyone's laughing at you. Salomão lowered his eyes and saw his wife walking through the kitchen, he remembered and envisioned his wife walking through the kitchen, he looking at her and she being different. When Salomão raised his head, he saw the devil going away, but his smile and gaze were still in front of him, inside him. Master Rafael and the apprentice arrived with the window. As if he were still in a daze, Salomão held the chisel and hit it with the carpenter's hammer to make the hole match the lines. Master Rafael and the apprentice began to anchor the window in the wall. Salomão apologized and said he had to leave. Master Rafael told him to have a glass of red wine and called the blind prostitute. Salomão no longer heard. The blind prostitute entered the kitchen without knowing or guessing why they'd called her. Master Rafael leaned out the window and saw Salomão disappearing down the street.

THIS IS THE ROAD THAT PULLS AND DESTROYS ME. The ultimate and only road. This path that isn't a road. This sky that doesn't bring silence but that screams it when the silence is unbearable. I think: perhaps I'm no longer this body I've become, perhaps I'm no longer this form inside this body, perhaps I'm already my dead self just suffering, with no will left, just waiting for unarriving death. And yet, on this cadaverous afternoon that unites and divides the world, I pass through something that I am and know. I'm moving toward you, Salomão. In your steps and in mine, I'm coming closer. And the weariness that seizes me frees me in my duty to keep going. Salomão. Your eyes.

WHEN THEY SAW AND RECOGNIZED EACH OTHER, the distance separating Salomão from the town was the same distance that separated José from the Mount of Olives, and neither one hastened his step. At the same speed, neither fast nor slow, they steadily walked, as if they saw only each other, as if they didn't see each other. They kept drawing nearer. The sun guided them along the same straight line. The stubble covering the wheat fields observed them. The cork on the cork trees stopped growing. Their features, dim and abstract in the distance, came into focus at the same time, for José as for Salomão. Neither carefree nor solemn, their faces were of two men looking at each other as if for the first time but without surprise or curiosity or useless words. They stopped. They were separated by exactly two steps: one belonging to José and the other to Salomão: exactly two steps. The two steps separating them were too small to prevent either one from imagining himself inside the other, from seeing himself with the eyes that weren't his and through which he saw. And in a fraction of the instant in which the world also stopped, Salomão looked at José, or José looked at himself. And in that silent gaze, larger and more forceful than a thousand words explaining each word of a thousand words, José spoke to himself, or Salomão spoke to him. He said it's not true, is it? And within himself, or within Salomão, José heard the question endlessly echo for a moment. José, or Salomão, lowered his eyes. Separated from each other once more, still in silence, Salomão almost smiled. They turned their backs to each other and drew away. Salomão reached the town before José reached the farmstead.

THE RICH PEOPLE'S HOUSE REMAINS. Empty. And full of what once was sincere hope and today is my dead gaze. The sheepdog sees me walk by without stirring. The yard is the same once I've passed it. The garden, small and yellow and hearty, doesn't feel me. I touch a gatepost of the pen, and the sheep look at me from the sleepy distance of their almost closed eyes. Behind the feed troughs, I take off my shirt. I grab the rope. I wind it around my fist. I hear it whistle. Like a sparrow. Like a sparrow whistling like a breeze blowing like a sparrow in spring. I switch hands. I hear it for a long time. A very long time. I put on my shirt. I go into the house. I look straight at the sun. I'm tired. I'm going to rest.

IT WAS ONE OF MY WORK DAYS
at the Mount of Olives, and in spite of Master Rafael's wedding,
I didn't want to miss, as I've never wanted and never missed. Old
Gabriel had told me the previous day it's all right if you don't
come tomorrow, and he was the one who paid me, for he had
been the steward ever since José's father had died. If this post
didn't bring him any benefit, it also didn't require much work.
He didn't have to contract laborers for the cork or the olives, nor
did he need to hire migrants for the harvest, since for thirty years
they were the same, working at the same pace, working up the
same dull sweat; and when a worker happened to die, his son
would take his place the following season. Nor did old Gabriel

have to keep any accounts, since for thirty years the same men would come on the same days to buy the same quantities of cork, the same amounts of wheat and olives, paying the same price as in previous years, and they'd return with the same measures of flour and olive oil, which were kept in the pantry in case the sons of Doctor Mateus showed up at the farmstead. And every year the vessels of old olive oil were poured out and filled with new oil, and every year the still-unopened sacks of old flour were replaced by sacks of new flour. It's all right if you don't come tomorrow, old Gabriel told me. But I had to go, as I'll always go, every other day, for the rest of my life.

That morning I'd already prepared the bath for Salomão and for my mother, I'd already dressed my mother, and now I was ironing Salomão's white shirt to take out the creases and the smell of moths, which came from its having lain in storage, while he pranced around the house barefoot, in his long johns and undershirt. He chewed on mint leaves and talked out loud. With a sprig of basil behind his ear, he said Master Rafael this, Master Rafael that. And he walked by me putting the chairs in place that were already in place, he washed his hands in the sink, nervous as if he were the groom, more nervous than if he were the groom. I put down the iron, and he came over and started dressing. All according to a strict order: after his underwear, then his socks, since they would be covered by his trousers; then his shirt, since it would go inside his trousers and under his coat; then his trousers and belt over his straightened shirttail and his smoothed long johns; then his shoes; then his coat. And this natural, logical order was only followed by Salomão on special days like that one, when he suddenly acted as if he were rich, as if every day he wore a fancy coat and had nothing to worry about except his daily and logical ritual of putting his clothes on in the right order, this being a distinguishing feature of his elegance and refinement. And while Salomão leisurely inserted an arm into one of his shirt sleeves, feeling its delicate warmth and pure white softness, leisurely imagining lands and estates, I crouched in a corner. I stuck a hand inside one shoe, spread a glob of polish on the toe, and vigorously rubbed with a cloth. While doing the other shoe I looked right at him, with no risk of being noticed, since he was buttoning his shirt with his head tilted back and his eyes closed. His shiny black shoes were in front of me, and I waited for him to finish tightening his belt. He slowly, aristocratically, pinched and lifted his trousers, sat down in a chair, and extended his feet. I loosened the shoestring of the right shoe and tried to slip it on, but it was very tight. I fetched the shoehorn. I wedged it between his heel and the shoe. I tried with all my might. I tried with all my might. I think I turned red. I couldn't do it. It was very tight. I stopped to think and Salomão, back from the wealthy lands and estates he'd imagined, pointed to the toolbox. I rummaged through it and found his carpenter's hammer. I put the shoehorn back in place, and hammered three or four times on the heel. I did the same thing for the other shoe. Salomão stood up and walked with comical footsteps to where his coat was. He put it on and no longer imagined himself wealthy and elegant, so painfully did his tight shoes rivet him in reality.

In ten minutes I was all dressed. I went and got my mother, who was sitting down, dressed in a crimson velvet dress and lace stockings up to her knees, looking like an orphan girl or a forlorn doll. We shut the front door and headed toward the church. The sun was the sun inside an oven. Holding her by the hand, I led my mother through the strip of shade next to the wall. Salomão, in the middle of the street, tried to keep up with his awkward way of walking, as if he were going up and down stairs. My mother, indifferent to the sun and to the morning and to the streets she seemed to see, repeated the words she always repeated. Whispering at great speed, she said more than five words with each step she took. And the older women marveled when they saw her, saying look, here comes the widowed cook, and they'd come up in pairs to talk to her, but my mother wouldn't look at them, she'd look down and keep on with her story, on and on, words; and the women, in unison or one at a time, would say poor thing, and let us keep going. When we arrived at the church, the only ones there were Master Rafael and the blind prostitute. She was grabbing onto his arm, and both were sweating. He wore a black winter suit and a heavy flannel shirt. She wore a simple dress and a white apron with a pocket in the middle and colorful embroidery along the bottom.

ON THE SAME NIGHT that Master Rafael spoke to her of marriage, the blind prostitute remembered the apron her mother had embroidered for her. Several days later, she took it from the chest where it nestled among blankets. She felt and smelled it. She slowly passed the apron across her face. And, all alone, she smiled as she had smiled more than twenty years ago, as a child, when her mother had given it to her, saying one day you're going to get married and you'll need this. And her mother didn't smile as she gave it to her, as her grandmother hadn't smiled, as her great-grandmother hadn't smiled, for they all knew that no man would want to marry a woman like that. And after they all finished making aprons for their daughters, they all destroyed the apron their own mother had made them, not because of an established tradition but because they'd run out of hope. And the blind prostitute could still remember the sound of the scissors cutting, the silent sound of the needle and thread passing through the fabric. And no one who saw the apron could ever imagine it had been embroidered by a blind woman, so accurate was its shape, so precise its embroidered letters: letters that had been copied from a towel given by Doctor Mateus's grandfather to the blind prostitute's great-grandmother, letters that were chosen because of the long loops in the *d* and *h* and the lonely dot over the *i* and that spelled dishes. When Salomão and his wife and the widowed cook arrived at the church, the blind prostitute and Master Rafael were waiting with their arms entwined, she discreetly running her hand over the apron, making sure it had no wrinkles. Salomão wobbled faster in his badly pinching shoes. Master Rafael's face looked younger. They exchanged a few words, as if exchanging a shared relief, and introduced their spouses. The blind prostitute and Salomão's wife silently and simultaneously pursed their lips, wordless and blind. The two men kept talking in the hot sun until the devil's smile filled up the area in front of the church. He stopped at the church door and smilingly searched his pockets for the key. Finding it, he inserted it in the lock and turned it with great force to overcome the rust. The hinges groaned a sigh, and his shoes crushed dry bits of dirt as they walked over the church floor. He was followed by the blind prostitute on Master Rafael's arm, by Salomão, and by the widowed cook holding on to her daughter's hand. The sound of the crutch and of footsteps approached the altar. In silence they watched the devil get dressed. The widowed cook and her daughter were the female witnesses and stood, respectively, behind Master Rafael and the blind prostitute. Salomão stood in the middle, as he was the male witness for both the bride and the groom. Having removed his cap and donned his chasuble, the devil blew the dust off the black book, smiled, and approached. And in the middle of his smile, words sounded. At first the wedding couple and the attendants tried to understand them but soon gave up, since they had never heard and couldn't understand them. And the devil's words drowned out the words that the widowed cook avidly repeated, repeated, whispering them in the echo. Cobwebs hung from the walls, weighed down by the dust and trembling when the devil raised his voice. The statues of saints, with their faces scarred by deep cracks, looked troubled. In one corner there was a glass case, coated with dried wax drippings and filth from the flies, that contained a huge hand truncated at the wrist and secured by wires. Its motionless fingers seemed to be grasping at something. Many years ago, when a certain coffin had been unearthed and its bones were being attended to, the hand was found to be still intact. The devil ordered the glass case to be made for it, and the word spread that a saint had been discovered. The earth had caved in on the coffin, and among the bones wrapped up in a bedsheet was the still-preserved hand. It was the hand of the giant. The devil washed it, used face powder to hide some teeth marks of dogs, used scissors to cut some long veins coming out of the wrist, and hung it from wires inside the case. He lit candles and left the church door open for a week. Since no visitors came, he blew out the candles, closed the church back up, and forgot about it. And there it remained, indifferent to the world and to the wedding, lit by the blue shadow of a small stained-glass window. When it came time to exchange rings, Master Rafael's left hand was of no use, for they had no rings. And the devil stepped toward their yeses, which no one heard, and told them to sign. They all signed with an X, and Salomão, who was the male witness for them both, signed one side of the page with two crossing diagonal lines, and the other side with a vertical line crossing a horizontal one. Salomão and Master Rafael left the church laughing. No one was waiting for them outside. Master

Rafael misjudged with his crutch and fell down the steps. Salomão helped him up and shook the empty knee and elbow of his suit. Are you sure you're all right?, he asked timidly, taking two steps backward, toward his wife. With almost no goodbyes, the newlyweds went hand in hand down the street that would take them home, Master Rafael swinging on his crutch, as the blind prostitute's head turned aimlessly on her neck. In silence Salomão, his wife, and his wife's mother also went home. The widowed cook, holding her daughter's hand, walked in the shade. Salomão went barefoot, carrying his shoes in his hand.

WHEN I REACHED THE MOUNT OF OLIVES, old Gabriel was surprised to see me. I told you yesterday that you could take the day off. Indeed he had. I'd taken a glass of water for him out to the yard, where my mother was spinning the endless wheel of her stories, which he pretended to listen to, and he said don't come tomorrow, you can miss a day. But I went. I knew that I had to go. I undressed my mother, removing and putting away the outfit she'd worn at the wedding; I dressed her, I put away Salomão's clothes, I got undressed, I dressed, I gave my mother her soup, put my scarf on my head, and went. I told you yesterday that you could take the day off. I didn't answer. And without paying attention to the questions he asked about Master Rafael's wedding, I looked at José's house. It was shut. The windows all shut. Old Gabriel noticed me looking and also stopped to look. Before he could say anything, I went into the rich people's house, and the coolness of the rooms and halls protected by old and thick walls couldn't put out the fire of that sun burning my body. I went to the kitchen sink made of marble and threw handfuls of water on my chest. With my eyes closed I threw handfuls of water on my chest. And I remembered being little. I remembered being little, six years old, and leaning into my mother, pretending that she was hugging me. I remembered hearing people say she practically raised herself, all alone. Alone. Alone. This, mixed up with José's face, was a crumpled pain inside me. Inside that huge and somber house, me a little girl with my huge and somber self. Me six years old, and the women left me bowls of soup on the doorstep, where my wild eyes would look out and retreat. She raised herself, they said. I found out later from old Gabriel, who told me without my asking, that for three years I didn't eat, that for three years I survived exclusively on the fat I had in my body. I found this out one afternoon, without having asked, when he came to see my mother and happened to mention it, as if it were normal. I didn't ask him, but he told me more, he said that when my ribs and cheekbones began to show, he started to bring me bunches of green vegetables and onions and potatoes and strings of garlic and jars of olive oil. And I, not yet four years old, would peel vegetables and cook and eat and wash dishes. I didn't ask him and would have rather not known, for I've never forgotten what it was like to have no one. Solitude. The big and empty house, dark at night. My mother next to me and alone, repeating her words over and over, like a breeze that never, never stopped murmuring, like a moan, like words that weren't words but something else that had the form of words and that was end-lessly repeated, like a sorrow. Yes, like a sorrow. My old mother. Almost dead. My mother far away from me. The dogs barking, the birds and voices in the distance, beyond the walls. My room pitch black and, beyond it, almost indistinguishable from a breeze, the soft sounds of the man shut up in a windowless room writing: his fountain pen circling on the paper, suddenly pricking it or crossing something out; his gentle breaths against the ink; sheets slowly placed over other sheets, sheets crumpled up and hitting the ground with the sound of eggshells. The shadows. The morning sun in the yard. And this, which was so little, was all I had until the day I met José. His gaze. And there, in the rich people's house, I once more filled my hands with water and threw it against my chest. And as I tried to feel some coolness, I heard the voice shut up inside a trunk, far away, alone. I slowly, silently approached. Sitting down in the main hallway, I still heard it say: solitude, death.

M Y HANDS. MY ARMS. THE SUN. I feel my arms open to the sun that floods me, that pierces me and is me. I feel my hands crucified in the light that flows and slides into me like a vertical river. I feel her gaze like this sun. My hands. Her gaze. The sun. And I know that my hands are still and silent and useless and dead. I know that her gaze doesn't see me. I know the sun is defeating me. The bedroom. The bed. I think: the place of men is a line drawn between despair and silence. And once more her gaze. Etched with fire on the inside of all that's impossible for me. As if the words I never told her were now shooting out from this sun and making my skin burn. Like a storm of voices. Like blades flying inside my body. In this light, the words I never told her. This sun which is my eyes' blindness and my knowing they're blind. And once more the bedroom. The blackness beyond me, which I don't see and I see, for I know it exists and know how its shadow awaits me. And her solitary, forlorn eyes also inhabit that blackness.

I slowly get up. I feel my hands, I feel the dark bedroom in my eyes. It's now morning of this day. How much time has gone by under the sun? No one knows. The days pass. I think: one day can be a thousand years. I think: no one knows if a day, a thousand years, or a fleeting hour has gone by in a day that passes. I slowly get up. I feel my legs, I feel the floor, I open the door. Next to the fire, my widowed mother. The black glow of her haggard and peaceful face. I sit down next to her. The mild heat radiating from the flames wraps me slowly, trying to hold me with its arms the same way it holds my mother. My widowed mother. We don't look at each other, and yet our gazes meet in the fire. Among the embers, our steady gazes look at each other as if for the first time. They bashfully touch over the tiny flame of a young twig. They reach out their hands. They feel each other's skin against their own. And the faces of our gazes plead over the fire, indifferent to the heat. They look at each other. They look at each other. And they understand the sorrows they tell, looking at each other. And in a moment outside time they slowly approach, like two trees that love each other, slowly, and embrace. Mother and son. I lift my head. My mother's gaze remains. I free myself from the web woven around me by the heat. I open the door. The dew is drying on the brown grass. The sun is rising from the earth. I look straight at it.

BEFORE LEAVING FOR WORK, Salomão stared long and hard at his wife. He stopped stirring the spoon in his coffee and looked at her, as if he suspected something. She turned this way and that, taking care of her mother's breakfast, looking only at what she needed next. Salomão continued stirring his coffee and then left for the carpenter's shop. He acted suspicious and suspected nothing. Only a week later, at bedtime, did he understand. His wife got undressed, he looked at her distractedly, then looked at her attentively, saying come over here, and he put his hand on her belly. He looked her in the face, and she almost looked at him. The widowed cook, like a dead woman who talked, slept and whispered her endless story to a corner of the bed. He slowly removed his hand from her belly, still feeling that figure, still with the shape of that slight mound in the palm of his hand and in his slightly curved fingers. He thought to kiss her but didn't, even though he had never had nor would ever again have a more fitting opportunity. Without moving he watched as she put on her nightgown, lit up only by the dim glow of the kerosene lamp.

The next morning he woke up before daybreak and was the first to arrive at the carpenter's shop. When he heard the sound of Master Rafael's crutch, he ran outside and announced I'm going to be a father before anyone could even say good morning. Master Rafael, who acted like a gleeful young man ever since finding out about the imminent birth of his own son, patted him on the back and smiled. And with that enthused smile, they walked together the several yards separating them from the gate. They worked all morning. Master Rafael didn't come near him again until shortly before lunch. He told the apprentice to go on home, relaxed his smile and said, amid the mist of sawdust that swirled in the shop and was slowly beginning to settle, I'm worried. Salomão, immediately sharing his concern, looked at him and waited. And Master Rafael told him that at night, when going to sleep, he would place his hand on the blind prostitute's belly and not feel the slightest kick, or any movement at all. And he'd stay awake listening to the night's every sigh. Sometimes, in his sleeplessness, he seemed to feel something, but when he concentrated all his sensations in his hand, he felt nothing but unmoving skin, and that previous moment when he'd felt something dissolved in his memory like dust. In the morning she would avoid him, ashamed. And her eight-month-old belly was no more than an inert mound.

I DON'T KNOW IF IT'S THE SILENCE that tortures me. The encompassing anguish of silence. The old sheepdog passes by and looks at me, and I don't feel her gaze. As I silently undo the wires of the gate, my hands feel nothing but silence and its vacant texture, its emptiness against my skin. I don't know if I've gone mad. Everything I desire is impossible in this silence. I think: the place of men is a line drawn between despair and silence. I'd like to be reborn, to start off fresh. But I continue. I follow the sheep, knowing each of their movements and feeling all of their weariness. And I slowly die. I'm vanishing with each movement of this world, which no longer has anything to offer me. I've become my own shadow. I've become a shadow of a shadow of a shadow of myself. I'm vanishing into time and silence. I think: the place of men is a line drawn between despair and silence. I'm slowly dying.

MASTER RAFAEL AND SALOMÃO went their separate ways on the streets leading them home. At that hour lunch was waiting for them amid the evasive glances of their wives. As they walked to their respective homes under the same sun, Master Rafael thought of Salomão's naïve joy, and Salomão thought of Master

Rafael's anguish. They crossed the threshold at the same time.
They felt the shade cover their skin with a coolness that dis-
agreed with Master Rafael but that was soothing to Salomão, and
they went back to thinking of themselves. Salomão sat down.
Master Rafael laid his crutch on the table and sat down. The
table was already set for both. The blind prostitute bustled about
the kitchen, dodging Master Rafael's veering head, whose wide-
open left eye tried to follow her motions. Salomão's wife ran between the widowed cook and the stove, stirring the water and
soup that boiled inside the pot, and making her mother comfortable in her chair. Both women put the food on the table at the
same time; both sat down at the same time. Salomão's wife began to spoon soup into her mother's panting mouth. The blind
prostitute calmly began to eat. Salomão and Master Rafael simultaneously opened their mouths to say something and simultaneously let their words dangle, unspoken, as they swallowed their
first spoonful of soup.

I LOOK STRAIGHT AT THE SUN. The trunk of the big old cork
tree slowly fuses with my back and turns me into wood. The
earth slowly fuses with my stretched legs and turns me into
earth. I look straight at the sun. My gaze is sunlight.

MASTER RAFAEL AND SALOMÃO looked at their wives at the same
moment and closed the door behind them. Salomão's boots,
touching the earth, kicked a stone here and there. Master
Rafael's crutch and boot, touching the earth, carefully avoided
the stones in their path. The sunlight smoldered on their skin.
Master Rafael tilted his cap. Salomão tilted his cap. Something
slowly died and something slowly lit up in both of them. Master

Rafael slowly began to remember Salomão's naïve happiness. Salomão slowly began to remember Master Rafael's anguish. And they met, as if they'd expected to, at the point where the two streets met. Together, without talking, they walked to the carpenter's shop.

DAWN. THE GRASS SLOWLY lifting. Rustling sounds from far away, farther than on other days, waking up like a very old man returning to life with his meager strength. It was Saturday, and therefore a different and special day. The sun, a ball of fire, appeared on the horizon later than on other days, pouring its unbridled river of flames across the streets and fields, burning what it had spared the day before. It was summer. In every nook and cranny a light was growing that only children could see. A gentle light that only illuminated. Dawn slowly took shape in the air and in the birds' keen eyes as a new morning. The sky was a transparent place that could only be seen, not entered.

They began as muffled moans against her pillow, soft moans smothered in the coolness that still filled the room with a translucent darkness. Then, when it seemed they had finished and the blind prostitute lay back and lowered her eyelids with a sigh of relief, she was seized by a new and stronger wave of pangs and anxiety, and the sun was risen, and Master Rafael woke up. He looked at her and felt frightened. With hair unkempt and looking almost ugly, she repelled him. He looked at her and felt frightened, not knowing what to do. During the night she'd kicked off the sheet, which lay balled up at the foot of the bed, like a worthless corpse. Master Rafael got up, got dressed, and, still frightened, looked at her again. The blind prostitute lay there half sunken into the mattress, on top of the badly wrinkled undersheet, with her belly sticking out, with her body all contorted so as to keep her belly upright, with her back arched to the breaking point. She was propped against two firm pillows, with her legs twisted and unabashedly wide open. Master Rafael looked and saw none of this, seeing only the tenderness he remembered. He saw a small and clean face that wasn't the one now sweating; he saw sweet and timid body movements that weren't those unruly ones. As if he'd closed his left eye for a moment, Master Rafael left the bedroom, went to the kitchen, and returned with a mug of coffee in his hand. He gave it to the blind prostitute and said you can't go with an empty stomach. Emerging from her pangs, she turned her head toward him as if she could see him and took the mug with her two hands. She raised it to her lips in silence. The first, slow sip was a long moment of peaceful calm. But she still hadn't finished the coffee, there was still a brown remainder in the mug, when she jerked forward without warning, leaving Master Rafael just enough time to place the basin under her mouth. And there he stayed, with the right side of his torso and the stub of his arm pressed against the blind prostitute's shoulder, and with his left hand holding the basin under her mouth. Unable to do anything more, Master Rafael stood still as she bellowed and vomited. When it was over, he wiped her lips with a towel and didn't notice the blood in the basin, threading amid the coffee.

Time was passing and, like a girl who leaves off being a girl, the morning slowly left off being morning to become a blazing fire that made the earth crack from within. Master Rafael, leaning against the window, looked at the yard through the chink between the shutters and remembered imagining a garden with trees and flowers or a cabbage patch. And that garden he'd only imagined seemed to him in that moment to be all the things he could have done. And the groans of the blind prostitute, growing in intensity or at least seeming to him louder and more frequent, were a refrain that tormented him. Looking through the chink between the shutters, as if his whole body had become his gaze and vanished into the earth, Master Rafael repeated lemon trees grafted into orange trees, apricot trees grafted into peach trees, grapevines, cabbages, flower beds with colorful patterns, lilies, mallows. It was a childish illusion which he shouted in silence to convince himself it was attainable, which he shouted in spite of an inner voice denying it, which he shouted so as to drown out that feeble, almost dying voice that said you've done nothing, that said you knew everything and did nothing, an agonizing and ruthless voice that would say these things whenever he found a silent respite in his inner darkness.

Drawing away from the window, he went over to her as if he'd just noticed her. He pulled up a chair and sat next to the bed. He looked at his hand that moved without moving, and placed it on her belly. The blind prostitute tried to smile. And

Master Rafael didn't feel any of the anguish or fear he'd been feeling for many nights. Looking farther back, he felt the same joy he'd felt when he found out he was going to become a father. A father. And that certainty, which he'd sometimes forgotten, became the only certainty. And it gleamed in his eyes. And the groans of the blind prostitute, which had tormented him with a cold terror, now seemed a natural and almost pleasant, soothing sound. A father. And his hand, resting on the blind prostitute's belly, told her all this, comforting her, and in this way they talked. The afternoon dragged on, like a life. And when the birds, free at last of the afternoon heat, began to fly over the yard that began to turn cool, when the blind prostitute tightened her face and it was clear she was about to give birth, they were both already old and loved each other still more.

Master Rafael stood up and ran to the window with his crutch as if he didn't have a crutch and opened it. Then he fetched two clean towels and a tub full of water and an empty tub. Because of the shame they knew they both felt, without ever having talked about it, he called no one. The light outside was fading and Master Rafael lit the kerosene lamp. The blind prostitute felt something rip through her like a blade, splitting and slashing her, as if her torso and neck and head had been sliced down the middle, turning her whole body into an open wound. And she struggled with all her might, as if trying to pull up a tree by the roots or to move the world over an inch. Her skin was purplish red and wrinkled. Her face was sheer suffering. Her water broke over the balled-up bedsheet, as Master Rafael didn't have time to put the tub in place. And the baby began to emerge just as the new day descended on earth and night still filled the sky. First the head. Master Rafael, knowing what to do, used two fingers to pull the baby by the roof of its mouth. It was born.

The turmoil ceased, like something already long forgotten. Rafael held up the baby, still covered with blood, and looked at it. It was a girl. His daughter. Blind in both eyes. Missing her right arm. Missing both legs. She didn't cry. She didn't move. She was dead.

And the girl's tiny corpse fit in his hand. His thumb and pinkie wrapped around her chest. His other fingers supported the head that hung from her neck. And the weight he felt in his arm was the weight of her dead life. He looked at her. Stared at her. And her glowing child's face, her lips, the soft shadow cast by her nose and the sockets of her eyes were like a self-pronouncement of death. And Master Rafael, filled with the blackest grief, was darkness itself. He slowly raised his head to look at the blind prostitute, stretched out on pillows, arms extended and hands open, with her nightgown striped by blood where her flesh was gashed. Peaceful, with a relaxed face, as if sleeping. Master Rafael nestled the child on the bed and bent over the blind prostitute. He placed his hand on her chest. Her skin tired, warm. Blood covered his fingers. He placed his hand on her face. Her skin. And he felt the image of her face, as she had once felt his. And his fingers slid through her sweat, leaving a trail of sweat and blood. He lifted his arm and waited for the form of her face to dissolve in his hand. The sorrow that remained: a silent absence of meaning falling on all gestures, an abyss negating the meaning of all words, a veil that canceled time. The woman he had truly loved, truly loved, was now nothing in this world. And his solitude was a sky even vaster than the night, a sky where there was nothing but night and cold, a black place he entered with his gaze. Leaning on his crutch, Master Rafael went to get the shawl that had belonged to the blind prostitute as a girl, and to her mother before her, and to her grandmother before her mother. It was a white shawl made of soft wool, its fringe dirtied by time. It was kept in a small chest, among other treasured objects: the apron from the wedding, a knitted wool coat, a flower-print scarf. He returned to the bed with the shawl and wrapped it snugly around the baby. He pressed her against his chest, placed her between her mother's arms, and covered them with a sheet up to the shoulders. He looked at them for the last time and left.

Night. It was a night of deeper, total silence, a night beyond silence. Master Rafael's footsteps, indistinguishable in the darkness, made no sound. The lightless and desolate houses, with windows and doors shut, were speechless blocks of stone that accompanied him for an instant but stayed behind, as if lost or abandoned. Prevailing over his weariness again and again but never definitively, Master Rafael walked on. His body, like a dead tree, or a dead morning, or a piece of death itself, walked on. His lips trembled. Sweat ran down his chest. A breeze silently swept over the ground. A breeze not felt. The baby girl's face. The blind prostitute's face. Master Rafael remembered. And each image he saw was an image of his endless solitude. The night in Master Rafael's gaze, beyond all silence, was a well with clean water where children played during the day without fear, throwing pebbles and imagining twigs to be boats; it was a well with clean black water, a solitary well, on a plot of land far from the town, on a moonless and starless night without end. The baby girl's face. My daughter. The blind prostitute's face. You were my certainty and I lost you. Night. Master Rafael went on. Up ahead, in the opaque blackness, he visualized the carpenter's shop.

He thrust his hand deep into his pocket and found the keys. He opened the gate, which for the first time made no sound, whether of rust, dirt, pebbles on the ground, or boards. He walked without stumbling in the absolute darkness, knowing the place of things that had places and the things that had none. He struck a match and lit the kerosene lamp. It was an old, soot-blackened lamp that was used in winter when night fell early, and the rest of the year was forgotten behind a box of crooked nails, where it impregnated the sawdust that fell on it with kerosene. He slowly made his way to the table in the middle of the shop and set down the lamp. Then he went to the window and opened it. The quiet song of the crickets filled the night's vastness with their absence. As if he were gazing at the sky, Master Rafael saw the baby girl wrapped in the shawl and nestled in the arms of the blind prostitute. Mother and daughter. He lingered on his vision of them. They slept and no one could harm them. He closed his eyes. He opened his hand and felt the blind prostitute's face. Her skin. Her hair wet with sweat. And he knew deep down that she was dead. Without looking back, he returned to the table in the middle of the shop and sat on one end of it. He looked around. The bench that had been his father's. The tools arranged in the way he always arranged them. His father working and teaching him. Patiently teaching him. With a simple, satisfied look in his eyes. Master Rafael tossed his crutch on the floor and it made no sound. On the floor, like a worthless object. And he raised his hand in front of his face. He looked straight at it. A thick hand, like either one of his father's. In the palm of his hand and be-tween its fingers he felt the weight of the little girl's corpse. My daughter. Her scrawny chest. Her tiny lifeless head. Her face. He grabbed the saw and held it against his leg. He aligned its teeth with the wrinkle where his leg joined his groin and began to saw, tearing trousers and skin at the same time. The blade dug into his flesh. Master Rafael kept his arm and gaze steady, as if he were sawing a board at a right angle. And when he sawed his leg bone, it made only a dull sound. Blood streamed down from the tabletop. His leg fell next to his crutch, like one more useless object. The baby girl's face. My daughter. Master Rafael stretched out his arm, grabbed the kerosene lamp and hurled it to the floor. Flames rose up the walls. And on that night the flames reached the sky.

I OPENED MY EYES. I HEARD
the shouts on the street but didn't want to hear. When they
banged on the door with their fists, I got up, still in my long
johns. They came in without me telling them to. In the kitchen,
darkly lit up by the small moon that shone through the open
door, they looked like ghosts with long whitish faces, ghosts with
bright and disembodied eyes, and they said the carpenter's shop
is on fire. I stopped looking at them, as if they'd said nothing,
and returned to the bedroom. I struck a match, which slowly ex-
ploded in the air. I lit the kerosene lamp. My wife sat up in bed
without speaking, her belly a growing mound under the sheets.
The widowed cook, her face buried in the pillow, which muffled

the syllables she formed with each breath, seemed to have fallen silent. Through the wall I could hear the sound of the fountain pen of the man shut up in a windowless room writing. It was the sound of thoughtless, impulsive, angry strokes. To someone who didn't know, it might seem like the sound of crossing out. But no, it was the sound of writing. I bent over to put on my trousers, first the right leg, then the left. I buttoned my shirt. With my face leaning over the lamp, I looked at my wife, who did not look away. The men's husky and nervous voices arrived from the kitchen. I blew out the lamp's small flame.

Only outside, when already halfway there, did I feel the cold shock of waking up and being real. The sudden awareness in me of myself. Of myself and of the world. The unspoken embarrassment of our being three men walking in silence, and the perhaps ridiculous hurry of our steps, and the ridiculous sound of our noses breathing. The faces of the men who had woken me up. Their solemn and unchanging expressions. The discomfort of cold clothes against my skin still warm from the sheets. A breeze entering through my shirt sleeves. And the deep dark night before dawn. The stars, likewise ridiculous, in the dull black sky. The three of us walking quickly, as if it were important. And then a halo of light swirling in the sky over the carpenter's shop, as if the sun were trying to come up in the middle of the night, to rend the darkness. And as we got closer and closer I remembered, as if struck by an idea, the peaceful gaze of Master Rafael, the open gate of the lumberyard, the declining afternoons seen through the window of the carpenter's shop, and I hurried my step even more. At last wide awake, by the time I reached the shop I was walking as if running, or running as if walking.

The rafters had given way and the roof, in two halves with the tiles intact, had caved in on the carpenter's shop. The flames rose up where the roof had been. Streams of sparks flew upward and vanished into the sky. The night swallowed up thick black waves of smoke. The gate was a pile of fallen boards on fire. A long row of men and women shouted and passed buckets of water from hand to hand. And they uselessly threw the water against the fire, as if it weren't water and the fire and night weren't fire and night. As if they poured empty buckets into the air, as if they hurled buckets of nothing against an indifferent fire. I stood there all alone and watched. The flames warmed my face, my flesh, my blood. No one had told me, but I knew that Master Rafael was dead. I looked and that's what I saw. And morning broke. With the first light of day the flames went out. The women went home. The men sat down on the ground next to me. I was the only one standing. The carpenter's shop had burned to the ground. Every strip of wood, every pinewood log in the yard, every speck of sawdust, every board, every unfinished window, every carpenter's bench, every tool. The walls, which no longer held anything up or protected anything within, were charcoal black. Amid the silence of the men and the morning, the embers crackled with a dim glow under the ashes, quickened now and then by an intermittent breeze. Old Gabriel loomed in the distance, coming toward us with his slow steps. He came up to me.

I DIDN'T SAY GOOD MORNING. I didn't say anything. I looked at Salomão and each man there, and each man and Salomão looked at me with the clear gleam of grief in their eyes. I looked at the fire. The last ember died out in a sigh that ascended as a small swirl of smoke in the air. One by one, the men started to get up. The last one came to me and said in a whisper, as if behind a shielding cloak, that when they learned of the fire they went to

Master Rafael's house and found the blind prostitute dead from childbirth, with the child likewise dead; he said that Master Rafael was inside the carpenter's shop; he said he was sure that Master Rafael was inside the shop; he said that Salomão didn't know. He stopped speaking to hear what I had to say. There was a brief silence, and then I waved him along with my hand. A few men searched among the ashes for things of value. Perfectly still, as if he weren't breathing, Salomão stood in the same place and in the same position, like a post, like a hill, like an unmoving tree. In his eyes the flames still raged.

OLD GABRIEL TOOK A STEP toward Salomão. The distant sun cast its first ray of light between them, separating or uniting them. Salomão knew what old Gabriel was going to say to him, and one could see in his face that he merely waited to hear it for it to become irreparably real. Old Gabriel, without disturbing the silence, used the same words the man had used, for in his one hundred and fifty years he had learned no words to say things besides the words that say them. Salomão looked up. The sky on that young morning was much bluer than he would ever have imagined. The heat was starting to set in. The day was starting off old and weary. Together Salomão and old Gabriel walked into the town. The first women, bent over, were sweeping the square of shade in front of their houses with small straw brooms, and they stopped when the men passed but did not look at them. The birds watched them in respectful silence. A slight breeze went with them. They walked for a long time that was no time and reached Master Rafael's house. The door was open. People were going in and out. Salomão and old Gabriel entered. The blind prostitute and the baby lay on the bed that was made up with a borrowed bedspread. Women had washed their bodies with a damp cloth. Their skin was smooth and peaceful. The blind prostitute had on her simple wedding dress and the white apron embroidered with the word dishes. The baby was wrapped in the shawl. Salomão, holding his hat in his two hands, looked at them from the doorway. The women had placed chairs along the wall around the bed early in the morning. The chairs all came from four neighboring houses. There were some empty seats among the women's black clothes and staring faces, and old Gabriel sat down in the chair at the end. Salomão kept looking at the blind prostitute and the baby, and only stopped looking to look nowhere and to walk without a word to where Master Rafael's suit was kept. He returned to the bedroom with the suit folded over his stretched-out arms and laid it on the bed next to the baby, as if Master Rafael were there in that empty suit. The trousers were brown and with the right leg folded and secured with a safety pin; the coat was gray and with the right sleeve folded and secured with a safety pin. Salomão removed the pins and pulled down the trouser leg, which was a darker brown, and extended the coat sleeve, which was a darker gray.

I DON'T KNOW FOR SURE if it's morning that's passing, afternoon that's passing, or all of life that's passing in this morning, in this afternoon. The sun's coming through the window we built on a Saturday when Master Rafael's eyes shone with even more light than can come through this window. The apprentice has already arrived. The boy's clever, Master Rafael had told me not long after he was hired, in a low voice so that the apprentice wouldn't hear. When he began he didn't know how to drive a nail, but he's clever, he'll learn. The apprentice arrived by himself, in his work clothes. He passed by all the people, and looked at me the same way he looked at Master Rafael's suit. I never asked his age, and I suspect that not even master Rafael knew it exactly. He's probably eleven or twelve. The boy's clever. I'd rather be sitting by him, but I sat down in the chair I was shown, next to these old women who sometimes try to talk with me, as if I could hear them. They say things like he was a good man, or she was a good girl, or the poor innocent baby, and they expect a response, which I don't make, and among themselves they whisper Salomão is so tight-lipped. The sun's coming through the window we built on a Saturday. A woman in black sees me looking at the window, gets up, and slowly closes the shutters, as if she were doing me a favor. Her friendly-looking face is a smile I forget. And I realize we're now shut up inside a frozen time. There is no more morning or afternoon or life beyond this dusky room. Only the dim light that comes through the front door, the kitchen, and finally into this bedroom lets us know that we exist here. We're the place where death resides. I'm the place where death resides. And yet when I remember Master Rafael, I can only remember him alive: looking at me, talking, telling me things. I remember him, but his invisible death weighs like a certainty over the place where all of this still happens, where Master Rafael looks at me, talks, tells me things. My memory of him is wrapped in fire. The carpenter's shop on fire. Master Rafael looking at me from the flames. Master Rafael working at his bench on fire with tools on fire. Master Rafael hobbling on his crutch through the shop on fire.

The shadow of my wife arrives, leading the shadow of the widowed cook by the hand. They walk past me as if they didn't know me or as if I were no one. Old Gabriel stands up to offer his seat, greets them at some length, and goes out to where the men are, standing around the door. Lots of men. Sometimes I hear the chorus of their voices saying good day to someone who enters or who's passing by. But the harmony they make is neutral, a sound of silence entering this bedroom like something that's already here. My pregnant wife looks at the blind prostitute. Both have the same peaceful skin. The widowed cook moves her lips, and although I know she's repeating her same old story, for the first time I don't hear her. I hear only a silence more silent than the breeze passing through the leaves of the cork trees, than the birds flying high up in the sky. An endless, relentless silence. I look at the lips of the baby who died before being born, and it seems like all the silence comes from her small and thin closed lips. A baby's small lips that know death.

I see Master Rafael in the places where he isn't, places that look sad without him. Sometimes we'd leave for lunch at the same time. We'd walk together down the street. I hear the thumping of his crutch. Before he got married, I'd hear his crutch at night going faster. He was going to visit the blind prostitute. And I'd stop what I was doing and go to the door just to tell him good evening, just to say see you tomorrow. In the late afternoon, early evening, when the light of summer turned the color of honey and settled on the plains, or when, in winter, the darkness of a starless night would fall over the town, I'd say see you tomorrow. And I'll never again say to him see you tomorrow. Never again so many things. Never again anything. He walks alone down the streets where we walked together. I stand still and watch him walk. He goes slowly, slowly, and disappears. I'm left alone, on a deserted street.

A COOL SHADOWINESS BLEW through the bedroom, grazing Master Rafael's suit, the baby's face, and the blind prostitute's white wrists. Outside, the hottest hour had pushed the men into a narrow strip of shade along the wall. The sweat from their bodies dampened the whitewash. And as if they were in Judas's general store, the men talked about the pastures and planted fields, about the properties of Doctor Mateus, and sometimes, if one of them remembered, they said a couple of words about Master Rafael, they said Master Rafael, followed by a vague, listless silence flowing from their eyes. At lunchtime some of the women left in the company of their husbands. Shortly before the hour when she habitually set out for the Mount of Olives, Salomão's wife also left, pulling along her mother and without saying goodbye. Salomão still remembered or saw her shadow vanishing at the threshold when José entered with a solemn air. His firm boots stopped in front of Salomão, who was finally able to cry, like an anxious child who had been waiting for his father or mother, and he started pouring everything out to José. José sat next to him and tried to calm him down. The widows looked on with wide eyes. When Salomão finally regained his composure, when his tears dried on his cheeks and his lips stopped moving, the afternoon returned, long and slow, like an afternoon that harbored death.

Old Gabriel came in and out of the bedroom repeatedly. He would come in and silently proceed to the last chair, walking past the silence of José and Salomão; then he would go out and stand like a quiet man among the men who talked. He came in and went out, marking time. And when the two wagons appeared at the top of the street, old Gabriel saw them arrive. The first was the funeral wagon, painted a shiny black, and it carried a small child's coffin, white and trimmed with gold lines. The second was Pedro's wagon, chosen because it was almost new and in perfect condition, and it carried the coffins of the blind prostitute and Master Rafael. Old Gabriel looked at the wagons approaching slowly. They came in a cool breeze brought by the late afternoon. They came in an ever-nearer, sadly clearer light. The birds flew in silence. The water gently trickled in distant fountains. At the house of Master Rafael they stopped. The men gathered around. The only sounds were of footsteps and meaningless noises. The funeral wagon was pulled by two men. Pedro's wagon was pulled by a young, scrubbed donkey. The men brought the coffins into the bedroom. Salomão, José, and all the women stood up. First they brought the coffin for the baby. A little angel's coffin. Salomão watched the baby girl being placed inside, and as they shut the lid to the coffin, her face was that of a living baby, a baby who was just sleeping, a beautiful baby. Next they brought the coffin for the blind prostitute. Two men hoisted her up, and her head fell slightly back, her hair touching the bedspread and then the bottom of the coffin. At last they brought the coffin for Master Rafael. It was made of good wood, as he would have wanted. Salomão stretched out his coat and trousers in the bottom of the coffin, and they hauled it away, no heavier than when they brought it. Salomão and José followed it out to the street. A crowd of gazing eyes and the sky. The coffins lay on the wagons, the baby girl in front, followed by her parents. And the procession began. Slowly. Salomão and the apprentice walked right behind the wagons. Down each and every street. Slowly. Past each and every house. Salomão kept walking, through each and every moment. Salomão kept walking and knew that the next day or the next week, or on some day yet to come, he would have to pass by the house of the blind prostitute and Master Rafael, and it would be an empty and abandoned house. Salomão kept walking. At the cemetery seven men carried the coffins: one man carried the baby girl, four men carried the blind prostitute, and two men carried Master Rafael. And the cemetery lay open before them. They wended through the tomb-stones, along the walkway of withered grass and earth. At the far end was a large grave, where they placed the three coffins, side by side.

He LOOKED AT ME WITH A SE-
rious air. He ran his fingers through his beard, as if to disentangle
it. It's all right if you don't go today, old Gabriel told me. He
looked at me with a serious air. The sun was out and many men
stood around the door of Master Rafael's house. My mother, not
understanding why we had stopped, pulled me by the arm. It's all
right if you don't go today, he said, and he smiled at my mother
as always. But I had to go. I sat my mother down in a shady spot
in the yard, quickly gave her some soup, and then, as I always
did, every other day, I took the road to the Mount of Olives, with
a scarf on my head. I quickened my pace when I reached the
gate. I turned the key and entered the rich people's house. I

passed through the empty rooms. The fireplaces all cold, the large empty chairs staring at me, the shadows of the furniture sprawling across the dim interior, darkness on darkness. I sat down in the main hallway and listened to the voice shut up inside a trunk. Its words echoed in the silence intermittently, as if spoken as they were remembered. At each pause, the previous sentence lingered on the walls, written on the whitewash with the color of whitewash. It said: it's coming slowly, but it's coming, and it will be an infinite day, an everlasting night, a frozen moment that won't be a moment; and great matters will be smaller than the pettiest ones, and greater matters will be yet greater because they'll be the only ones. I didn't understand this saying from the voice shut up inside a trunk until today, when I woke up. Today, as the first and still-feeble light fell across my bed, I heard these words in my head. I heard these words, understanding each one, and I woke up. I slowly sat up under the sheet. I looked at my mother, I looked at Salomão. I lowered the sheet and looked at my belly, at my son who won't be born. Death seemed to me a simple thing. In the morning light that deliberately deceived me, death seemed to me a suffering equal to that of living, gazing upon a new day, knowing everything I know.

My mother was the first one to open her eyes. And for her, waking up meant only that: to open her eyes, to suddenly open her eyes without changing her expression, to open her eyes and keep on with the next word of her story. Salomão slept the heavy slumber of dejection for not having found a day laborer's job or any kind of paying work. I slowly lifted my mother up by the arm, dressed her, and led her to the kitchen. I gave her some coffee. And I wanted to talk to her. I held her face between my hands. And I said nothing, since there are no words for calling her. Mother. Death is that solitude from where you don't see me, where we're not together. And I wanted to say mother. But I could only look at her, I could only see the silence of the word mother in the clear and cool air, in the empty kitchen inhabited by our two solitudes. And I gave her my hand. The skin of her rough fingers furrowed by knives that had cut potatoes into strips, that had chopped collard greens and sliced melons. Their bones deformed. Her hands I know so well and held so often, where I find some slight warmth and longing. And I sat her down in the yard. I sat her down in the same shady spot as yesterday and every day. I brought her the miniature pots and pans and silverware for dolls. And I stayed and watched her. She grabbed a clump of grass, collected drops of dew inside a tiny pot, gathered a pile of pebbles and another of pure dirt. Then she carefully mixed portions of dirt, grass, and dewy water. The morning was far from her and far from me. In the mounting heat I watched her, as if I hadn't already seen her and it weren't just a painful memory. Behind me the bedsprings groaned with the wearied sound of Salomão getting up.

The kitchen walls were the sad and faint reflection of the morning's light and innocence. From yesterday's dishes, turned upside down to dry, I grabbed a pot for lunch. I acted as if preparing the food were of the utmost importance. Standing there, making useless motions with my hands at the usual speed they worked, I watched Salomão from out of the corner of my eye. Disheveled and unshaven, looking anxious, with his shirt misbuttoned and half out of his trousers, and his belt too loose, Salomão stumbled into the kitchen like a man drunk on brandy, searching for my gaze with his wide-open eyes, like a helpless soul. And whenever his face came within a foot of my eyes, I pretended to be looking for an onion, or wiping up a drop of oil, or picking up a potato peel from the floor. Salomão, who was never

mine, whom I only felt sorry for but who imagined he was mine,
since he had always imagined he was someone's and had never,
since childhood, let his actions be themselves. Salomão, in the
kitchen, like a body without a body's substance, like a thing, like
a body that was a breeze or a silence, like a piece of a person: an
innocuous voice, a dull gaze: a piece of a person that had seen itself suddenly promoted into a whole person, with full responsi-
bility and a full quota of suffering. And in the sharp clarity, as the
boiling water lifted the potatoes and I felt I was literally boiling
within, in the moment when the walls were walls and everything
seemed to be exactly what it was, with everything definitively
existing at each instant, I looked at Salomão, who was looking
steadily at me. Eye to eye, as if we saw each other. And in his
gaze or in my gaze, I found what we might have been, were it
not for life: the tiny moments we would have deemed greater
than these and greater than all moments, since we would have
known no others. And in that clarity, as I began to take notice of
Salomão, of his face and his shoulders and his arms, the whole of
him began coming undone: the skin on his face started cracking
like parched earth, coming loose from his flesh and dripping
thick blood; and in that red blood, in the bones poking out from
beneath his flesh, his eyes kept looking at me, larger and with the
same weakness and the same innocence. It was like death, like
dying. I lowered my gaze to Salomão's unlaced boots, and when
I looked back up, I saw his face intact and his eyes suspended in
the same fragility, like a woman or child on the verge of tears.
But I knew it hadn't been an illusion of my seeing, I knew it for
certain, I knew it was the world's ultimate clarity. I drew closer
to him. I stripped him, as if I were stripping an image or a statue
or a child, and in the bedroom I picked out some freshly washed
and ironed clothes. A pair of trousers, a white shirt. And time

mercifully seemed to enlarge to become the moment when we were most together, in which all our tenderness converged and all our gestures asked forgiveness for what wasn't our fault. I dressed him in the white shirt, which was still smooth on his body, I dressed him in the trousers, placing two coins in one of the pockets, I slowly tightened his belt. I sat him in a chair and, amid the light and shadows, I patiently and carefully and affectionately combed his hair. And as I opened the door for him, as I saw him walk past me, knowing he would go to Judas's general store, as I saw him grow smaller in the distance and vanish at the end of the street, I knew for certain that it was the last time, I knew that never again, never again would we meet.

I didn't sit down. Still standing in the kitchen, with my gaze fixed on nothing, as if fixed on the horizon, I felt a hot breeze that brought with it all the sounds of the backyard, that outlined my body inside my dress and that took it a little farther, like a flag. I placed my hands on the small mass in my belly and thought it was death inside me. I have death inside me. My gaze and the breeze stopped. Slowly, overcoming the force of grieving hands present in each movement, I crossed the kitchen and stabbed a potato with the fork, and it was already cooked through. With the fork and the wooden spoon and with profound resignation, as if it were a task for the condemned, I mashed the potatoes in the soup. And my feet stepped to the back door, from where I watched the sun's rays passing through the leaves of the trees and piercing the shade all the way to the ground. Delineated, well-defined sun rays, like those that penetrate the quiet water behind dams and also become water, perfect rays of luminous water. And amid the peacefulness I heard the song of the sparrows, the scattered and harmonious noise of the sparrows, like a distant silence, still tolerated, still allowed by the morning's mild heat, and the uninterrupted whispering, the infinite whispering of my mother, like a sound from earth, like a sound from the beginning of the world. I drew near to my mother, to her body hunched over something, to her flaccid, old-woman's body. She was hunched over a figure she had sculpted. I drew nearer, to see. And it was me. That face made of soil and small stones and grass was me, as if it were made of skin. It was me. Those hands calmly resting on the figure's belly were mine, with the fingernails and lines across the knuckles in perfect detail. It was me. I lifted her up and we stood there, mother and daughter. With the morning all around us. I took her hands. She didn't look at me, but for the first time in my life I was certain that she saw me. I know that my eyes betrayed a grief as large as the morning, an invisible grief, in the moment when the invisible was all that could be seen. And time was that moment multiplied over and over. Our hands clasped over and over, reaching out in front of us and with our arms ending at the same place where our hands were clasped. Our gazes over and over, with their weight like the world, like the earth and the static gesture of things existing. And within that vast time there existed the word mother, as if it had never existed before. The word mother that I didn't say, but that was. Mother. I took her into the kitchen. I sat her down in a chair. Slowly, one by one, I removed the pins of her hair bun. I let down her long and smooth, gray and white hair. I untangled it with long strokes of the comb until it fell over her shoulders and down her back. I ran my fingers through her hair. I felt the strands slipping through my fingers. I redid her hair bun. Her face looked cleaner and younger. I gave her something to eat. Spoonful by spoonful, as if I were counting them and saying one two three. As if someone were secretly and silently counting them, so that they seemed inexplicably counted. I fed her the soup until the

204

spoon clanged against the bowl, which I tilted to scoop out the last drop. I washed her face and dressed her. I brought her some clothes that looked like new, all washed and ironed, some nice clothes. A skirt and a blouse. I dressed her and took her into the bedroom. In between her lips' mumbling, while I made the bed, I noticed that the faint sounds of the man shut up in a windowless room writing had grown yet fainter and slower, the ink sticking to the paper with the languid sigh of a flower, as if the words had suddenly taken on new meanings. And I again took my mother's hands into my own. Our gazes were made of silence. The silence was death. I laid her down in bed. I positioned her head on the pillow. I pulled her feet together. I joined her hands on top of her chest. My mother against the white sheets. Purity. The air like cool water on her skin. The clean whitewash of the walls dawning perpetually. My mother, a girlish mother, mother, a childish mother, skin, girl, mother. I stroked her face gently, as if I weren't touching it, and, without touching it, felt it. I looked at her. I looked at my mother for the last time, and I left her there. Mother, as if you were just resting, as if you were just waiting for sleep to arrive. Mother, how I'd like to have held you in my arms, how I'd like to have been held by yours. For you death isn't cruel, mother, since you died to everyone a long time ago, since you only kept existing to remind me of love, and now that nothing in me can turn back, now that I'm sheer vertigo, your mission is finished and you can rest. Farewell, Mother. Thank you, silence. In the kitchen I placed the scarf on my head and tied it around my neck. I went out without looking back but imagining the cool shadows, the noises that would arrive from the street for no one at all to hear, the kitchen forlorn and forgotten, like a coffin beneath the world.

The sun weighs on me like something I carry within. I carry

the sun inside me and calmly pour out all its light and heat over the fields. It's too late to turn back, since there's never any turning back. Only the regret for what we didn't choose persists, exists. Only the old age of the cork trees, the sculpted shape of the olive trees, stones suspended in the sky and in this earth crossed by the flight of birds, this earth, the world's age and clarity, my eyes that are the sky and the cork and olive trees, my eyes that weep without weeping, this road I've walked a thousand times and a thousand times it's the same, I, I and the sound of the earth, the crunching of the sand under my feet. And I walk on as if standing still, I feel as if I sometimes force my legs to stop, I feel them standing still, and yet I walk on. Despair and the end are approaching. And despair and the end, now I know, are the serenity of an eternal and irreparable solitude, they're a grief that's an eternal and irreparable suffering, everything eternal and everything irreparable, they're the silence of someone crying all alone on an infinite night. The Mount of Olives isn't far and I see old Gabriel. I feel my legs walking, I speed them up, I try to flee, but I'm standing still in front of him. He looks at me for years and years and says don't go. I'm suddenly old like him, I feel the enormity of his life in that gaze that is set on me and says don't go. He says don't go, and the sun tortures him even more. There's not a breeze or a cool moment in his face. I turn from his gaze and go on. Time doesn't belong to me, nor does life, or words, or the water of springs and fountains. And old Gabriel, more than his face, is a gaze that knows everything, is the name of solitude talking to itself, is the word death suffering its own fatal torment. He's more than his face but is also his face, his sorrow, and his tenderness. More than his shadow, he's also his shadow. His childish gaze full of certainties. His fear. Behind me, an instant. Old Gabriel, crushed by a hand or by a mystery or by a secret, falls dead on the ground that knows him, that knew his one hundred and fifty years but that doesn't remember him now that he's dead. His body, lying on top of the earth, his grave, his dead body, visited by sparrows that happen to alight on his chest. His body, like a furrow of plowed land beneath the sun. His dead body shouting all the silence of his solitude across the sky, down the road where I go on, over the fields which are the world. And the day's hottest hour immortalizes this death and its splendor, immortalizes death, and each moment is this infinite death in all places. And I go on. I go on. I place my hands on my belly, on my dead son. I carry death inside me. The sun shouts the vastness of the fields and my sadness. In the depths of my gaze and inside me, I see the farmstead. I go on. I'm solitude.

WHEN I WALKED PAST MY WIFE and felt the sun in her eyes and realized that my legs were walking on the street without knowing where to, it was as if my body were nothing but its own weakness. Since I knew she was looking at me, I walked as straight down the street as I could. Then I stopped and leaned against a wall in some shade. No one passed by, not even a dog or a chicken. Only the pigeons, as if they were free, traced wide arcs in the sky, imperfect circles. Only the pigeons passed by all morning, but without looking at me. I felt a finger choking my throat and making me want to vomit. I lowered my head and made sounds of vomiting, felt my stomach emptily churn, opened my mouth, stuck out my tongue, and vomited only the nothing I'd eaten that day. Straightening up, I looked at the hazy image of the world. At the indifferent sky, the indifferent houses, the indifferent existence of things. And I kept going. Wherever my body took me, without knowing where I was going. The silence was perhaps an audible murmur, perhaps an insistence that kept repeating a despair, a disquiet, whose speechlessness and anxiety made it all the more anguishing. I was my own uncertainty. I was that moment, and that moment was the fascination of one who looks on without understanding. I was the empty place of myself, I was my eyes, I was my gestures that were no more than my absence. And I kept going. I kept going. Wherever my body took me. Down the streets, an anxiety and a discomfort. My life happening independent of me, without me directing it, without me existing. Me without me. I without I. Me, and someone acting in place of me. My hands stronger than my will. My legs walking without being mine. And the silence shouting at me, saying all that I didn't understand, or know, or listen to. And the morning's poison made me cross the square. Looking normal, like any man in any banal moment, like a man not carrying a world of suffering in his shadow, on a morning just like other mornings, I crossed the square and entered Judas's general store and lowered my gaze. And Judas's general store, which would have been cool on a normal morning, cool like the shade, was the heat from outside and the sun and the light and the men looking at me and the devil smiling and a glass of red wine in front of me and the counter burning with heat and my skin seething with sweat and the devil in front of me smiling and the men looking at me and the light and sun and my legs like rubber and the flesh of my arms shriveled and my arms like dead weights and my face in front of my face as in a mirror and my face defeated and worn and old and facing death and the tempter facing me to say your wife and smiling and saying José and smiling and saying the two of them and smiling and saying like rabbits and smiling and saying him on top of her and smiling and saying like rabbits and smiling and the glass of wine making me hotter and the light and the sun and death and death and death

208

and the devil smiling and saying José and smiling over and over and over and over. Judas's general store would have been cool on a normal morning. Judas's general store would have been cool like the shade. Judas's general store was the heat from outside. It was the sun. It was the light. The men looked at me. I drank a glass of red wine. The devil smiled. The devil smiled and said your wife is with José, the two of them together, like rabbits, him on top of her, screwing.

And I walked through the streets as if seized by a rage with no cause. And I walked through the streets carrying a weight that, I now realized, was a profound grief. I felt inwardly abandoned. Banished and lost inside myself, with an inexplicable rage, with a profound grief. I am death and don't know what death is. I am sorrow and dejection and torment and don't know. I'm my not knowing anything and this suffocating anguish, endless and suffocating. I walked through the streets and arrived here. I arrived here and arrived nowhere, because I'm the same. I'm on the road that goes from the town to the farmstead, and I'm still at the square, I'm still at Judas's general store, where the devil smiles at me and says like rabbits. The sun striking the earth scorches me, and it wouldn't scorch me any less if I were walking in the sky, nor would I feel less anxiety. The sun striking the earth scorches me. The silence saddens me. The infinite vastness of the wheat fields saddens me. And the sun above the sun, inside the sun, overlaying the sun, the sun, the sun, the sun's heat is my luminous grief, my sorrow, the news of my death announced to me and my sadness. I'm where I haven't arrived. Here I keep walking, I go on. The olive and cork trees, August, the turned earth, the earth's smell. My wife and José are this heat and my legs walking. Or perhaps they aren't. Perhaps I am this heat I don't control. I am my legs that walk without me. I am this

anguish much larger than me. I am eyes that see me. The road
that continues. I am ears that listen. The sand under my feet. The
sand under my feet. The road that continues. I see old Gabriel.
His night-ravaged face veiled by sadness and discouragement.
And I hear old Gabriel. Don't go, his voice dying, don't go, his
feeble insistence, don't go. I look at the pleading in his eyes. I feel
his tender, sick-child's gaze. As if I didn't see him, as if I didn't
hear him. And I keep going as if I'd thrust a knife into his voice,
as if I'd turned him into nothing. Behind me, the silence of his
slumping body. Old Gabriel dead. His life of one hundred and
fifty years yielded up through resignation. Behind me, old Gabriel's
sad and resigned death, and sad because resigned. Behind me his
certainties, lost forever, scattered across the earth, in the wind and
in the light of the sun. Over the wheat fields looms the devil's
smile saying him on top of her, the two of them going at it like
rabbits. The sweat on my face is the sweat of a thousand men.
My face is a thousand faces. The world has shut down. Nothing
exists in the distance, behind the hills. Here, as there, all that exists is my despair and desolation. In the depths of my gaze and
inside me I see the farmstead. Alone. I'm solitude.

THE SHEEPDOG EMERGED from the midst of the sheep as if she
were one more sheep, coming over with her belly full of stubble
to look at me. Her eyes, large with earnestness, spoke tenderness
and comfort. She also knew. I called her with my gaze and ran
my hand through her fur. She lay down at my feet, feeling those
moments which she knew, she also knew, would be my last. The
big old cork tree grew even larger above me, and then the sky.
And the vast plain, vaster than a spring breeze, greater than all
the heat I felt at that hottest hour of the day. On either side, behind me, in front of me: the world. This is how I ended up. This

is me. I think: it's coming slowly, but it's coming, and it will be an infinite day, an everlasting night, a frozen moment that won't be a moment; and great matters will be smaller than the pettiest ones, and greater matters will be yet greater because they'll be the only ones. I think: it's today. And the silence that once seemed innocent to me, that same silence, now seems to me cruel and murderous. I run my hand through the sheepdog's fur. The sheep obliviously graze. And my eyes blackly look upon death. The trail of suffering left by death before it arrives. Its certainty. And this anguish more powerful than any power is choking me. I know, and this knowing gives me everything and takes everything from me; it makes me a man and shows me death; it teaches me, forcing me to forget. And I feel that the sky's roots, planted in the ground, are planted inside me. I feel, I feel it as I feel the sun falling on me or as I feel my hand in the sheepdog's fur, but I know that the sky isn't mine. I know. Not even death is mine. Just my own death. I'm distressingly small within myself. And I, within myself, am all that I am. I'm small and insignificant, I'm a past history of misunderstandings and mistakes, I'm the act of gazing at this sky, I'm the certainty of no future. I find the smell of the earth in the heat, and I smile with my lips and in my gaze. Never again. My smile is sad. It always was. Smiling, I laugh at myself and cry for myself. No one cries for a man whose gaze is black like this. I cry for myself, without tears. My dry eyes uselessly look at the sky, my dry face burns in this day's hottest hour, my dry lips smile and cry with self-contempt. I run my hand through the sheepdog's fur. I find the smell of the earth. Deep earth, mother and core of the world. I think: why?

I raise my hand and the sheepdog, waiting for this moment and knowing it to be the right one, looks at me with all of her eyes' pity. Without my whistle needing to tell her, I see her round up the sheep and drive them toward the farmstead. Beneath my black sheepskin and beneath my shirt, what's left of me impels me onward. At each step, I thrust my staff forward. In a long and slow arc, it strikes the ground and I pass beyond it, as if I were always, always passing myself. Onward I walk, and I remember her and remember Salomão and remember my mother. In the same whirling thought: her, Salomão, my mother. Her sad gaze, Salomão's childish gaze begging please, my mother's gaze of death and mourning. Onward I walk, and with me, within my steps, sitting still by the fire far away from here, my mother also walks. Her waiting for death where she always remains is her way of walking in time. And only in time can we walk. Even if our feet tread the ground, as mine seem to do, only in time can we walk. Right now she's gazing at the fire. The fire that gently burns. Forever gently. In the slow combustion of a heart engulfed by a gentle suffering. Gentle and incessant. A fire of suffering oppressing her heart. My mother who knows and gazes at a secret, who sees death in that secret, who gazes at the fire and sees me. Mother, your waiting is almost done, but not your suffering. I think: not to exist, to be the forgotten thought of someone forgotten forever, to repeatedly die when already dead. The sheep are my silence walking ahead of me. Salomão, my cousin whom I never called cousin, the son of my father's sister, Salomão, the frightened little boy who would come around and confuse cork trees with olive trees, suppose that thrushes were swallows, and call the sheep as if calling a dog, holding out his closed fist saying come get your treat, Salomão, where are you now? Where did life lose you? Where did life lose us both? I think: not to exist, to be the forgotten thought of someone forgotten forever, to repeatedly die when already dead. And her. Woman. Promises. Her face. I never lied to you. If I said sky to you, it was sky. If I said sun or water, it was sun or water. If I said morning, it was the morning of your eyes deceiving me. Without your eyes deceiving me. The deceit of a morning that was born in your eyes. We dreamed. We dreamed and were blind. And I'm not afraid of the word love. I'm not afraid of words. Look how I say death: death death death death death. By repeating it so much I take away its meaning. I take death away from death. I take away darkness and solitude. Death death death death death. I'm not afraid of words. Once more I see your eyes before my own, morning, and I want this to be our last word: love.

And I keep walking on the road to the Mount of Olives, I continue, I go on. The heat. The earth. The sheep the size of my shadow. I see old Gabriel. He looks at me with anguish. I keep walking, I continue, I go on. I'm in a hurry. He says don't go, with his voice the same as when I was ten years old, he says don't go, I remember sitting and listening to him for a long time, don't go, that important voice, don't go, if I could I'd sit down and stay with him, as I did when I was ten and the sun shone on us with its last rays and living wasn't a sad thing. Don't go. I have to go. I'm in a hurry. I keep walking, I continue, I go on. Behind me old Gabriel dies on top of the bare earth. Lifeless old Gabriel is the earth. I'm in a hurry. Never again the trees. Old Gabriel. Never again the earth. I'm in a hurry. Everything waits for me where I don't exist. Nothing exists anywhere that I'm not, and I'm not anywhere. Everything waits for me to destroy me yet more. I'm in a hurry to reach a conclusion. I'm in a hurry to disappear. Up ahead lies the Mount of Olives, the sun. I keep walking, I continue, I go on. I'm solitude.

*A*ND THE WORLD ENDED. INEX-
plicably, or without an explanation that can be stated and understood. The world ended, like a shutting of the eyes in which not
even the things we see with eyes shut are seen. The children died,
and with them their laughter, scattered in the sunlight and on
Saturdays and in August. The world ended, as if swallowed by a
night descended from heaven, and never again was the laughter
of children heard, never again was it Saturday, never again was it
August, never again was there sunlight. And this absence of the
world wasn't even an absence, it wasn't even the empty space
once occupied by a person who died and which you can look at
and which exists when you feel it. It wasn't even an absence, be-

cause there was no one to feel it. It was an infinite night concentrating all the fear of all nights since the first night of the world. But not even fear existed, because no one existed to feel it. The place of the trees, their shapes and their thoughts had died. The streams, their cool water, the barely audible sound of their cool waters, the streams had died. The sprawling fields, the dry leaves, the stones lost in the ground, the vastness of the fields, the wind over the earth, the fields of wheat stretching as far as the eye can see, the earth had died. The houses with their whitewashed walls had died. The birds in flight, their late-afternoon chirping, had died. There were no more afternoons, mornings, evenings. Never again would the day slowly dawn with blurry eyes; never again would anyone sit and dream of peace in early evening; never again would the night drift over houses, covering them with its star-studded cape. The world ended, and not even time continued. The minutes didn't pass because they didn't exist, even as no moment and no gaze existed. Infinity was the infinity of not even being infinite, nor anything at all. Amid all the dead things death didn't exist. There were no cadavers. The memory of death had died. The children had died, which was the only thing worth crying over, but no one cried, for there was no more sorrow, no more tears, no more eyes, and no breast for crying. José and his mother, Salomão and his wife, the devil and the widowed cook had all died, among all the men and women who had died, like specks of a gigantic multitude all dying at the same instant without anyone realizing that they were dying and that everything was dying. Everyone disappeared, leaving nothing behind, not even the tiny nothingness that exists in the nothing that exists in nothing. They didn't even leave behind the cemeteries full of corpses, since these all disappeared even more than everything else, all having died their yet more definitive, second death. The voice shut inside the trunk ceased forever, with neither the meaning nor the silence of its words surviving. The man shut in the windowless room writing stopped short in mid-sentence, and the end, for him, was the ink disappearing from the pages he had lived, it was the sheets of paper fleeing from themselves and becoming the most absolute void of all, it was memory transformed into less than air, less than wind. The world ended. And nothing remained. No certainties. No shadows. No ashes. No gestures. No words. No love. No light. No sky. No roads. No past. No ideas. No smoke. The world ended. And everything was a blank. A blank smile. A blank thought. Blank hope. Blank comfort. Blank gaze.

A NOTE ABOUT THE TYPE

The text of this book is set in the digital version of Dante MT, designed by Giovanni Mardersteig after the Second World War. Drawing on his experience from using Monotype Bembo and Centaur, Mardersteig created a new text face with an italic that would work harmoniously with the roman. Originally hand-cut by Charles Malin, it was adapted for mechanical composition by Monotype in 1957, and the new digital version was redrawn by Ron Carpenter, also for Monotype, issued in 1993 in a range of weights. Though originally designed as a book face, Dante can also work well in other formats such as magazines and newspapers.